Jacky Warwicker is a retired drama/performing arts teacher living in North East England.

Through writing, she has found a new way of communicating with an audience. Her stories illuminate the courage of people scrambling through upending change. Using varied settings and compelling voices of all ages, they champion the importance of human connection.

In addition to exploring places of cultural interest, Jacky enjoys going to the theatre, reading and walking.

For the young people in my family.

Use your talent, make your mark.

Jacky Warwicker

In Every Season

AUSTIN MACAULEY PUBLISHERS™

LONDON • CAMBRIDGE • NEW YORK • SHARJAH

A CIP catalogue record for this title is available from the British Library.

ISBN 9781035851331 (Paperback)
ISBN 9781035851348 (ePub e-book)

www.austinmacauley.com

First Published 2024
Austin Macauley Publishers Ltd®
1 Canada Square
Canary Wharf
London
E14 5AA

Special thanks to Mick, my walking, talking and writing companion.

Chapter 1

Perdy stepped out of the brilliant sunshine into the dampening shade of the cabin. Adjusting her eyes to the darkness, she scanned the barren room for fast-moving spiders. '5,000 miles from home,' she said with a sigh. *A long way to travel to avoid a family showdown.*

The buttery sound of her neighbour strumming a guitar filtered into the room. She visualised a Joni Mitchell lookalike until a rich, tenor voice burst into song. A crescendo in the performance suggested it was for her, the newly arrived counsellor from England.

Perdy knocked on the wall to signify her appreciation of the cool rendition.

'Something good has begun,' her neighbour sang with ear-catching verve.

'I hope so,' Perdy called out, as she collapsed supine onto the bed.

Much to her delight, the musician began playing a medley of sweet-sounding chords. On the edge of sleep, she imagined him as a curly-haired angel watching over her from afar.

Perdy stood by a group of girls gently massaging each other's backs on the lawn. In a rare moment of ease, she watched the light dance across the inky blue lake. *Why have I buried myself away in stifling lecture rooms for so long?* she asked herself. *I don't want to be an imposter shackled to a medical degree.*

Then don't be, an inner voice said tartly.

Outwardly happy, Perdy counted the good-natured children as they shuffled into line. A young boy, positioning to be her favourite, ran forward and placed his tiny hand in hers. He smiled impishly as they stepped onto the yellow track leading back to the cabins.

'We're off to see the wizard,' the boy said, stiffening his body like the clunky Tin Man.

'The Wonderful Wizard of Oz,' Perdy sang, imagining she was the tremulous lion seeking courage for the future.

At the end of the trail, the children slid indoors away from the mauling heat. 'Bye campers, see you in the morning,' Perdy called out, craving the serenity of her own cabin.

With the characteristics of Tigger, Rocco bounded towards her with a beaming smile on his face. In a buoyant mood, he began his usual tomfoolery: 'Oh goddess, nymph, perfect, divine! To what, my love, shall I compare thine eyne?'

Drawn to his zest like a moth to a flame, Perdy joined in: 'O spite! O hell! I see you are all spent to set against me for your merriment. If you were civil and knew courtesy, you would not do me thus much injury.'

Delighted by her recall of the bard's comedic lines, Perdy threw herself onto the grass. 'Beats studying medicine,' she said, as Rocco sank down beside her.

'Doesn't compete with saving lives.'

'I got pushed into it by my parents, I'm not cut out to be a doctor.'

'Stick at it, you'll be a great medic.'

'I'm leaving my course,' Perdy announced, 'I just haven't told anyone yet.'

'Really, why not?'

'A case of my parents living through me, they'll be devastated.'

'It's your life, everyone needs a raison d'être.'

'I did my best,' Perdy said, 'I've had to come to terms with my limitations.'

'It's a breakthrough, not a breakdown.'

Hearing the laughter from the swimming pool, Rocco leapt to his feet. 'Let's go skinny dipping tonight, under the silvery moon,' he suggested.

Horrified by his madcap idea, 'I need to catch up on some sleep,' Perdy replied.

'Tomorrow night then,' Rocco urged.

'We'll see,' Perdy said coyly.

In the Metropolitan Museum of Art, Perdy scrutinised Chagall's radiant painting of the "*Lovers in the Lilacs*". Empowered by their tender love, the couple lay blissfully happy in a gigantic bouquet of flowers. The man with ebony black hair caressing the head of the half-clad woman reminded Perdy of Rocco. Distressed that summer camp had ended, she thought about her impending loneliness without him. *Part of me will always be skinny-dipping with Rocco in the lake under the watchful moon*, Perdy mused. Deliberately discounting the existence of his girlfriend, she pictured the two of them as the idyllic lovers cradled in each other's arms.

Perdy walked slowly through Central Park in order to delay her dreaded departure from Rocco. In a world beyond camp, she saw him playing his guitar to a crowd of people near the fountain. Unable to face a painful farewell, Perdy twisted on the spot like a dancer trapped in a box. Tenderly, she blew a kiss in Rocco's direction and imagined it falling on his colourful bandana. 'Bye dearest friend, thanks for a brilliant summer,' she said from the core of her heart. Then mustering all her strength, Perdy turned away from her soulmate to start travelling without him.

Chapter 2

Pleased to get a window seat on a crowded bus, Perdy rested her head on her crumpled hoodie and closed her eyes. In a quickly descending dream, she found herself trapped in a cell draped in beady-eyed stethoscopes. Desperate to break free, she tried to yank them down but they coiled around the bars like sinuous snakes.

Nudged by a fellow passenger, Perdy woke startled from her fleeting nightmare.

'You alright?' asked a girl with lavender hair and sharp brown eyes. 'Only you called out like you were in pain.'

'Just a bad dream.'

'Got something on your mind?'

'Parent trouble,' Perdy said, suspecting she would understand.

'My mum died when I was seven and my dad's my best friend so I can't help you there.'

Perdy marvelled at the girl's sunny disposition despite her sad loss.

'I'm going to soccer training in Pittsburgh. I want to be a professional player, as great as Meghan Rapinoe,' the teenager announced.

'I'm visiting distant family,' Perdy said, feeling like an interloper.

'They'll be thrilled to see you.'

The girl's unbridled optimism hit Perdy like a blast of fresh air. 'I'm looking forward to meeting them,' she found herself saying.

Perdy sat in the garden drinking a cold beer with her cordial relatives. Proud of their English ancestry, they had welcomed her like a cherished daughter.

'Our great grandmas were sisters, is that right?' she asked Stan, trying to establish their relationship.

'Yes, they were incredibly close before Freida came to America.'

'Such bravery, leaving everything behind to start anew.'

'We have her diaries. A priceless record of family history.'

'I'd like to read them sometime.'

'Just to warn you, she lost a son in the Vietnam war so they're harrowing in places.'

'Poor Frieda, what a tragedy.'

Perdy watched the gleaming wet children from the pool race across the lawn. *Healthy descendants of a GI bride and an American soldier*, she thought, happily.

'You don't seem like a doctor,' Stan said, taking her by surprise.

'What makes you say that?' Perdy asked.

'Too dreamy,' Stan said with a smile.

Perdy saw herself in the lecture room, remote from the other students locked in steely concentration. She recalled putting down her pen and turning to the pallid grey wall, lost in turmoil. 'I've got a lot on my mind,' Perdy said.

'You need a good holiday. I'll take you out on my boat tomorrow.'

'That will be wonderful, cruising the waters of a glistening lake.'

In the balm of twilight, Perdy opened the first of Frieda's leather-bound diaries. The beautiful, stylish writing so different from her own medical scrawl, tugged at her heartstrings.

When Joe jitterbugged into my life, I didn't expect to be following him to America with all the other "wallflower" brides, she read, sidling into Frieda's world.

Hope mam doesn't regret making me such an eye-catching dress to wear at the dance. She didn't foresee me launching into marriage and abandoning Blighty for a new life halfway across the world. Despite my calm resolve, her uncontrollable sobbing at the train station filled me with guilt. 'We're going to miss you,' Mam cried out as she grabbed Dad's arm to steady herself in a throng of well-wishers. At least I managed a brave smile as I waved goodbye to my valiant clan.

Perdy thought of her own mother awaiting her return from a foreign land, unaware of the distance growing between them. Lured back to the past, she continued to read Frieda's compelling story recorded in the family heirloom:

Joe's cheery, relaxed manner did more to brighten the drabness of war than his supply of luxury gifts. Not to say these weren't treasured: the eggs, the nylons, the flowers but he was the standout prize. With his bubbling affection, impeccable manners and shiny shoes, Joe stepped into our war-weary hearts.

Perdy read details of the Queen Mary's turbulent journey across the Atlantic, transporting war brides to the promised land:

I don't know which is worse, homesickness or sea sickness, both are tossing me around in this sprawling ocean. Fortunately, listening to the band playing in the elegant ballroom is a soothing diversion. There's a real camaraderie when everyone joins in the tender singing.

Immersed in Frieda's story, Perdy turned to the page which recorded her arrival in New York:

With all the other women, I rushed on deck to catch my first glimpse of the Statue of Liberty, bathed in light. Seeing the awe-inspiring sculpture gave me a rush of hope for my new life in America. When the girl from the Red Cross called out my name, I walked down the gangplank and saw my beloved Joe with his arms outstretched, waiting to greet me.

Knowing that Frieda's hope had turned to despair, Perdy searched for the entries chronicling the Vietnam War:

Our beautiful son, conscripted and sent to a living hell. Slaughtered in bloody combat alongside thousands of doomed soldiers. Coerced into war; forced to sacrifice his life in the viperous jungles of Southeast Asia. For what? To stop the spread of communism by supporting a government trying to defeat the irrepressible Vietcong? 'What passing-bells for these who die as cattle?' in the darkest of nights.[1]

My darling Robert, proud to wear his soldier's uniform, blown apart by rocket fire, thousands of miles from home. Oh, how I yearn for the greenness of England, away from this rampant insanity.

Perdy marvelled at Freida's strength: *In a world far removed from the dance hall, she battled through a maelstrom of pain to pave the way for future generations.*

An incredible lady, Perdy said to herself as she closed Frieda's diary.

At the bow of Stan's boat, Perdy perused the puffy white clouds in the cerulean sky. She made a mental note of the vista for her mind's eye to revisit on duller days. Being outdoors for most of the summer, she had attuned to the exhilarating power of nature. As the speed of the vessel increased, shooting them across the water, she felt a billowing surge of delight.

'A world far removed from stifling hospitals,' Perdy called out.

'Have you been in a speedboat before?'

---

[1] Wilfred Owen, *Anthem for Doomed Youth*, originally published 1920.

'Sadly no, too busy working to enjoy myself.'

'Work hard, play hard, that's my motto. Hope you've brought your swimsuit.'

'I have,' Perdy said, captivated by the quivering sheen of the lake.

Never, a strong swimmer, she wasn't tempted to compete with Stan's water prowess. Instead, Perdy pushed into the breaststroke, synchronising the frog-like movements with graceful ease. Feeling the warmth of the sun on her back, she closed her eyes and drifted into thoughtless bliss.

The piercing cries of a mother summoning her daughter from the lake caused her to panic. Thinking she was the object of attention, Perdy lost control of her strokes and sank deep into the ruffled water. Petrified of drowning, she streamlined her body and kicked hard to propel herself upwards. Gasping for air, she resurfaced and saw the mother swaddling her daughter tightly, like a newborn babe.

'Perdy, are you alright?' Stan called out in alarm.

'Just having some fun,' she said, swiping the tangled hair from her face.

He swam around her playfully before diving underwater towards the boat. Perdy raced after him, determined to break free from the shackles of maternal love.

Chapter 3

Under the umbrella shade of a Maple tree, Perdy carefully penned 'Howdy folks' on the fragile airmail paper. Keen to start her letter with good news, she described the serenity of the lake draped in golden sunshine.

A hummingbird, ruffling the stillness of the afternoon caught Perdy's attention. Like a suspended, multi-coloured jewel, it vibrated mid-air above the wind chimes. She wanted to hold the exotic creature in her hand; stroke the emerald green feathers coating the tiny body. With rapidly beating wings, it zoomed across the garden, effortlessly changing direction. Aware of her own stagnation, the thrilling agility of a bird in flight filled her with awe.

Upbeat about the possibility of a new, adventuresome self, Perdy strolled up to the house to get a drink. Hearing the hushed cadence of private conversation, she halted behind the door.

'Perdita means lost, which highlights the miracle of her being returned to her parents.'

'Pat didn't carry her own baby.'

'No, knowledge of Perdy's existence came out of the blue.'

'How did the mix-up at the IVF clinic come to light?'

'The birth mother was Afro-American, partnered with a Jamaican man, they knew the baby wasn't theirs.'

Perdy wanted to charge into the kitchen and slash through the roots of the pernicious gossip.

'There were tests presumably to ascertain the real parents.'

'Yes, a wondrous surprise for Pat and Neil who believed their embryos had been defective.'

'The mistake could have gone completely undetected. What a devastation for the other couple, did they fight to keep the baby?'

'No, they handed her over, despite their anguish.'

Perdy recoiled at the compassion in their voices which laid bare the truth of the tale. The ruby red head of the hummingbird intensified in colour as she slumped to the ground. Knowledge of her parents' secrecy wrapped around her like a strangulating umbilical cord. She thought of her birth mother blissfully carrying a baby in her belly, unaware of impending tragedy.

Feeling disorientated, Perdy shivered in the warmth of the sun. Belatedly, someone closed the door through which the bruising past had shunted into the present. Hugging herself tightly to contain the pain, Perdy resolved to find her own identity based on truth.

The tingling sound of the wind chimes seemed to applaud Perdy's decision to quit medicine. No longer thirsty, she raced back to the discarded letter to impart her critical news. Reverting to her usual scrawl, she quickly wrote the words which would turn her parents' world upside down.

Startled by the sudden ringing of her phone, Perdy put down her pen to take the call. 'An unusual time for you to ring Mum, is anything wrong?' she asked.

'Yes, darling. Stan called me, he said you might have overheard him talking to Helen about your birth.'

Perdy's deliberate silence amplified the tension. 'I did,' she finally said.

'It must have been awful for you learning about the mix-up in that way.'

'It was. I can't believe you and Dad didn't tell me.'

'I'm so sorry angel, there never was a right time to disclose the trauma. I meant to share everything with you when you were eighteen but Grandma's death overwhelmed me.'

Perdy wanted to rant about how selfish her parents had been but her mother's pain crackling down the telephone mollified her anger. She considered the lack of pregnancy photos and rehashed birth stories. 'A harrowing experience for you all,' Perdy said.

'I was gifted with a beautiful daughter; poor Fayola lost the baby she carried.'

Perdy felt a beating connection with her birth mother, 'Where's she living now?' she asked.

'Fayola moved back to Brooklyn when her marriage ended.'

'She's here, in America?' Perdy queried, contemplating the strange twist of fate.

'Are you alright sweetheart?' her mother asked.

'Not really,' Perdy managed to say. 'I'll call you back later.'

Stan stepped from the kitchen doorway into a ribbon of light shimmering on the lawn. He walked briskly over to Perdy and held out a bottle of beer. 'I thought you might need a drink,' he said.

'Thanks,' she replied in a quavering voice.

'I'm sorry you overheard the conversation; it must have been a real shock.'

'It was the worst possible way to find out about my birth. Why did my parents hide the truth from me?'

'They buried the past to seize the future.'

'And disregarded my rights.'

'Don't be too hard on them, they're loving parents.'

'I'd like to meet my birth mother; she lives in Brooklyn.'

Stan looked at the name and address headlining Perdy's notebook, 'Fayola Walker,' he said delightedly. 'She's a famous sculptor, a devotee of Augusta Savage, the first African American woman to open her own art gallery in America.'

'Remarkable,' Perdy said, moulding the achievements of both women into a single thought.

'Augusta founded the Savage Studio of Arts and Crafts, a training ground for African American artists who exhibited in her Salon.'

'A trailblazer for Fayola,' Perdy said. 'What strength my birth mother had to come back from personal tragedy and establish herself as a renowned sculptor.'

'You must have seen photos of "The Harp", Augusta's most famous artwork. It celebrates the first line of the Black national anthem, "*Lift ev'ry voice and sing*".'

'Guess Fayola joined the choir.'

'Pay her a visit, I think she deserves it.'

'She certainly does, nurturing me for nine months.'

Exhausted by the day's events, Perdy fell asleep fully clothed. In her dream, exultant choral voices rang out as Rocco somersaulted through the air. With great precision, he raised his hands to silence the musicians. Hearing a baby cry, Rocco climbed to the top of a tree to lift her from a cradle.

As two mothers swam around in a sea of tears searching for their offspring, he threw a young woman into the air. She plunged headlong into a never-ending void before opening her celestial wings to fly away. Deep in the dream, Perdy stretched from a foetal position into the untouched space surrounding her.

Chapter 4

Following Stan's instructions, Perdy turned into Westbury Avenue, looking for Fayola's brownstone house. The multi-story buildings, shaded by lacey-leaved maple trees, stood tall and proud.

Like some dystopian nightmare, my birth mother unknowingly carried someone else's baby, Perdy thought as she climbed the steps to Fayola's door. Eager to meet the esteemed artist, she knocked loudly to announce her arrival.

Fayola, resplendent in a vibrant orange dress, smiled with her whole being when she saw Perdy. 'My darling girl,' she cried out, 'what a blessing you're here.'

Swept up in her strong arms, Perdy felt the power of her embrace. When Fayola finally let her go, she spoke from the heart: 'I've been excited to meet you, I owe you so much. Thank you for bringing me into this world.'

'What a momentous day,' Fayola said, misty-eyed with emotion. 'Let's take a stroll in the garden before celebrating our reunion.'

In the tranquil oasis adorned with variegated grasses, Fayola walked amongst her sculptures as if mingling with friends. 'Every day I sang sweet songs to you, nurturing you in my belly but when I saw your flaxen hair and alabaster skin, I knew you were not mine to keep,' she said.

Lost in intertwined thoughts, they moved to the arbour seat trellised in jasmine. Perdy took Fayola's sinewy hand, prompting her to speak again. 'Six, two-hour visits took place before I kissed you goodbye. Your parents brought pillows so you could get used to their smell; Pat made a recording of her voice for you to listen to.' Fayola stayed steady as if recounting someone else's story: 'So many tears; layers of love wrapped around a priceless daughter.'

Hit by the pathos of events, Perdy pictured the harrowing scene related to her birth.

'I've come to terms with my infertility,' Fayola said, 'my sculptures are my offspring.' She gestured to the statutes ensconced in foliage, depicting America's past. 'Work gives me purpose, art is a way to fight racism and make progress,' she added.

Perdy scrutinised the sculpture closest to her, a hunched slave on the auction block waiting to be sold. *A powerful evocation of inhumanity*, she reflected, grasping the importance of Fayola's vocation.

A unique terracotta baby umbrellaed under the shadowy green ferns caught Perdy's attention. Fayola lifted the cherub from her grassy nest. 'My first work when my hands were learning to sing the blues,' she said. 'It's a sculpture of you as a newborn, take it as a keepsake.'

'She's beautiful, let her stay here, where she belongs,' Perdy replied.

Fayola looked into her eyes like an earnest mother. 'What inspires you?' she asked.

'I'm still searching for my raison d'être, Perdy by name, Perdy by nature.'

'It's not easy for young people these days, they have so much pressure heaped on them, it's a wonder they can breathe. Discover what makes your heart sing and you will find your way.'

'You've played such an incredible part in my life; I won't forget you.'

'You will always be precious to me, my English rose,' Fayola said. 'Let's go inside and toast to your future.'

Perdy sat on the hostel bed clicking her pen until a random flow of ideas impelled her to write. Enlivened by meeting Fayola, she jotted down insightful notes about her time in America. When keywords pulsated with meaning, Perdy searched for a cogent thread to pull them together. Fully absorbed in the task, she explored a range of ideas before moulding her poem into shape. Deeply satisfied with the finished outcome, she decided to ring home.

'Fayola's an incredible woman, it was inspiring to meet her,' she told her mother.

'I'm sure it was a special reunion for you both. We got your letter by the way.'

Expecting her mother to be horrified by her decision to drop medicine, Perdy girded herself for a blast of parental outrage.

'I wish you'd told us earlier that you were so unhappy. It takes courage to change direction but your wellbeing is all that matters,' her mother said.

My mum isn't angry, just 100% supportive, why does marauding paranoia stalk me at every turn? Perdy asked herself. Holding back the tears, she summoned the courage to speak her truth: 'I hope you don't think I'm being weak but I'm not doctor material. I'm changing to English and Creative writing, I'll send you my first poem, it's called "*Mothers*".'

'I look forward to reading it, sweetheart. What an exciting development for you.'

'Thanks, your support means a lot to me.'

'Dad and I miss you, when are you coming home?'

'My flight's booked for September 17th, I'll be back in time for your birthday.'

'A double celebration, we'll toast to the sunny days ahead,' her mother said.

When the call ended, Perdy felt upset that her parents were so far away, yearning for her return.

Astounded by the sound of Rocco's voice in the lobby, she jumped off the bed, sending her notebook flying. *Something's wrong*, Perdy thought as she raced downstairs to greet him.

'Wow, I didn't expect to see you so soon,' she said, giving Rocco a massive hug.

'I got your mind-blowing message about Fayola.'

'So much has happened since I last saw you, I feel like a different person.'

'Lucky for you having two mothers.'

Perdy noticed Rocco's burgundy rucksack slung sideways in the corner of the room. 'Change of plan?' she asked.

'I'm going to stay with my brother in The Bronx. Jade finished with me; she wants the freedom to do her own thing.'

'Perhaps she craves the adventures you've been enjoying,' Perdy suggested.

'She's taken the dog,' Rocco said, bursting into tears.

Perdy didn't know if he was more upset about losing his canine companion or his girlfriend. 'Fight for custody,' she said, trying to lighten the mood.

'I bloody well will,' he replied with uncharacteristic belligerence.

'At least you've got your guitar,' Perdy consoled.

'I'd be lost without it,' Rocco said, picking up his beloved instrument.

When he turned to face her, Perdy was saddened by the look of sorrow in his eyes.

'Everything's gonna be alright,' Rocco sang soothingly, as if he'd read her mind.

Chapter 5

Perdy was surprised to see a beady-eyed chihuahua peeking out of Rocco's jacket.

'My turn to look after Rita,' he said proudly.

'I thought we were going into the jazz club.'

'We are. This pooch loves music.'

'You mean you're going to smuggle her in?'

'She's not cocaine, Rita's a groovy amigo.'

Perdy rolled her eyes in disbelief, *not the evening I'd envisaged, dancing with a dog in a basement bar.*

'I can't miss this gig, Mom's playing the flute and Mica's on drums,' Rocco said.

'A musical family, very impressive.'

'They're also race equality lawyers.'

'A high achieving family, where do you fit in?'

'I'm going to make my mark in journalism,' Rocco said.

'Good for you,' Perdy shouted over a blast of music coming from an outdoor speaker.

Much to the surprise of the bystanders, Rita peered out from the coat and gave a long drawn-out howl. Before the watchful doorman could berate him, Rocco skedaddled around the corner with his canine friend.

Perdy followed him into the abutting avenue lined with berry-blue wheelie bins. 'Nice try,' she said, laughing at Rocco's clown-like solemnity.

'Mom's going to be heartbroken if I'm not there, she's playing a Cherokee song in memory of Dad.'

'I'm sorry, I didn't realise. Go and support her, I'll take care of Rita,' Perdy said kindly.

Rocco lifted the dog from his coat and placed her on the pavement. 'Thanks, you're a lifesaver,' he said, kissing Perdy on her reddening cheek.

Her heartbeat quickened as she watched him race boyishly to join his family. She thought of her own parents, crossing the days off the calendar until she returned home to England.

Perdy walked towards the park where she'd seen the athletic skateboarders earlier in the day. A teenager riding on the back of a homemade tandem waved nonchalantly in her direction. His sudden chuckle alerted her to the fact that a crisp packet had hooked onto Rita's snout like a muzzle. Bending down to remove the litter from the dog's nose, Perdy heard the loud jingle of an ice cream van in the vicinity. Enticed by the thought of a waffle sundae, she tied Rita's lead to the railing and waited for the vendor to park in the designated bay.

At the front of the queue, talkative twins were debating the merits of various popsicles. To curb her impatience, Perdy pictured Rocco's beaming face as he listened to his mum's performance in the club.

'Sorry about that,' the vendor said as if he were responsible for the twins' dalliance.

Perdy placed her order swiftly and turned around to check on the tethered dog. 'Oh, my God, Rita's gone,' she gasped, 'I tied her up next to the lamppost, someone's taken her!'

'Did you see a couple of teenagers riding by on a tandem?' the ice cream seller asked.

'I did,' Perdy said, perplexed.

'They do it all the time, take dogs for a ride in their cycle basket.'

'Barking mad, no pun intended.'

'Don't worry, one lap around the park and she'll be back where you left her.'

'Madness, don't the police stop them?'

'They've got bigger things to worry about round here.'

'Thank goodness she'll be returned.'

'Enjoy your ice cream,' the vendor said with a smile.

Perdy paced anxiously back and forth, nibbling the caramel cone. *What if the teenagers disappear with the cherished chihuahua, how will I break the news to Rocco?* she asked herself.

The unnerving sound of a toddler having a tantrum diverted her attention towards the kiddies' swings. Behind the fence edging the playground, she saw Rita being paraded around the park like canine royalty.

The teenagers pedalled the tandem up to the railing in perfect harmony. 'Bonkers,' Perdy uttered as she watched them ruffle the dog's silky brown fur. Before she could reach the flighty boys, they tethered Rita to the fence and made their getaway.

Thrilled to be reunited with the tail-wagging dog, she recalled the Kenyan women who had their babies stolen, never to see them again. Courtesy of Rocco, she knew about

31

the shadowy thieves who stole newborn infants from homeless mothers in Africa. His voice rang in her ears: *'Innocent babes are sold for paltry sums of money to pitiless buyers. The mothers aren't seen as sympathetic victims of crime, their story must be told.'*

Perdy waved to the ice cream seller giving her the thumbs up and sat on a restful memorial bench. With Rita snuggled safely on her lap, she watched the sun slip away from the streaky red sky. *Rocco's playful and profound in equal measure,* she thought, *I'm lucky to have him in my life.*

Perdy felt a frisson of excitement when she saw his man bun bobbing up and down in the throng of people. Immediately Rocco noticed her and the chihuahua, he quickened his pace to be by their side.

'I hope you've had a fun time looking after lovely Rita,' he said, kissing the dog.

'Eventful,' Perdy replied, 'I'll tell you about it later. How was the jazz concert?'

Rocco sat down close to her. 'Mum was tremendous,' he said, 'I recorded her recital on my phone.'

Perdy listened to the haunting, silvery sound of a flute reaching into the air. A rich melody shifted from note to note before scaling upwards to a high-pitched lament. In the celestial love song, Perdy heard the pain of a bereft lover calling a soulmate. 'It's beautiful,' she told Rocco. 'A moving tribute to your dad.'

'Absolutely, he was a great man. I'm going to the Catskills tomorrow, his favourite place, would you like to come with me?'

'Yes, please,' Perdy said, overcome with happiness.

Chapter 6

With his bandana wrapped around his shiny black hair, Rocco looked like an Indian Chief. 'At least the dognappers returned Rita,' he said. 'Imagine having your baby stolen, never to see her again.'

'Like the Kenyan women,' Perdy replied.

'Most of the infants are sold to childless couples but some are used for sacrifices.'

'Do the traffickers know this?'

'They don't care as long as they get their money.'

'Why doesn't the government do more to help the women?'

'Because they're the underbelly of society.'

'Whose story must be told!'

'Hope I'm not mansplaining you.'

'You're not. I wish more people had your compassion.'

A companionable silence settled over the conversation as they approached the forest. *This beats exploring the city hotspots*, Perdy thought as she scrutinised the natural beauty around her. Narrow rays of sunlight prised through the trees, brightening the interlaced ferns on the ground. Beneath their fronds, rotting bark gave shelter and sustenance to tiny living creatures. Happy to be by Rocco's side, Perdy breathed in the pure air of the peaceful woodland.

A high-pitched whistle above them heralded the sight of an epic wingspan gracing the sky. Rocco removed the binoculars from around his neck and graciously gave them to Perdy. She watched the massive Golden Eagle soar in elevating circles towards the heavens. With feathers spread like fingers, the imperial bird hovered deftly over the forest before swooping down out of view.

'Wow! Such majesty,' Perdy said, gazing into Rocco's deep brown eyes. He beamed with delight as he took the field glasses from her shaky hand. To regain composure, Perdy concentrated on the white-noise burble of a distant waterfall.

Spindly birch trees twisting through the relics of a 1920s hotel caught Rocco's attention. 'Indigenous people linked through culture and blood were removed from their land by colonists,' he said. 'The tribes in the Catskills were hospitable, they valued inclusivity and freedom.' Perdy contemplated the appalling brutality of invaders ousting them from their ancestral home.

Rocco stooped down to caress the trunk of a fallen tree. 'One of my dad's favourites,' he said reverently. Perdy knelt beside him and touched the shaggy bark of the Red Maple strewn across the path. Rocco placed his hand over hers, making her heart flutter like a fragile butterfly. 'Thanks for coming,' he said, 'I wanted you to see this place.'

'It's beautiful,' Perdy affirmed, resting her head against his shoulder.

From the tree, Rocco salvaged a brilliant red leaf and dropped it in her lap. 'A token of my love,' he said, putting his arm gently around her waist.

At the summit of Overlook Mountain, with intertwined hands, they watched the mist shift rapidly from the forest beneath them. On a scale Perdy had not seen before, a timeless expanse of land stretched to the distant river and beyond.

Rocco perused the scene in venerated silence before lifting his arms to the crystalline sky. 'This spot was identified by Native Americans as home to great spirits,' he said, 'I can feel them around me.'

Redolent of a tribal warrior, his voice slipped into a hypnotic chant, charging the atmosphere.

Perdy imagined hordes of displaced ghosts flocking to their sacred resting place.

Energised by his mantra, Rocco sprinted over to the fire tower and began climbing the steel frame. Perdy watched him mount the lofty structure with graceful agility and strength. Nearly at the top of the lookout, he swung fearlessly from the frame with one hand and blew her a kiss.

'Be careful,' Perdy cried out, alarmed by his high-spirited jinks. Overlapping her warning, Rocco hollered her name in long, protracted syllables with his rich tenor voice. Enraptured by the courtship ritual, she gazed adoringly upwards, like Romeo under Juliette's balcony.

'Come and join me,' he cajoled, reaching out for her untouchable hand.

'I don't like heights,' Perdy yelled at the cruel moment Rocco lost his grip and lurched forward. Frozen in terror, she watched him contort his flightless limbs and plummet to the ground. His head smashed against a jutting boulder, making her scream aloud in woeful agony.

With a palpitating heart, she rushed to Rocco's side and lifted the bandana from his head. Quickly, she used it to stem

35

the flow of blood from his angled neck and checked his pulse. Alarmed by his stillness, 'Come on Rocco, come on Rocco,' she pleaded over and over.

Carefully, Perdy eased his jaw forward to open his airways and moved him onto his back. Protecting his head with her sweatshirt, she interlocked her fingers over his chest and began the compressions. 30 in quick succession before pinching his nose and covering his open mouth with hers. Feeling the tightness of the seal she exhaled powerfully, inflating his chest upwards. Her life force flowing into his, she blew again, emptying her lungs. Like a skilled medic, she repeated the rhythmic compressions: 20, 25, 30. As dark blood trickled down Rocco's neck, Perdy fought with every fibre of her being to keep him alive.

Chapter 7

Rocco left this cruel world with our future tucked under his wings, Perdy lamented on the second anniversary of his death. She recalled the words of remembrance she wrote for him when her life fell apart:

The great spirits in the sky swept you from my arms and took you home.
Sweet summer friend, in every season of my life, you will be part of me.
From afar, your love resuscitates my failing heart.

Just as she was about to burst into tears in the newsroom, Tom stepped over to her desk. 'You wrote an impressive piece about the Kenyan baby thieves,' he said, in a congratulatory tone. 'Sickening that hospital workers were involved in the trafficking.'

'And kept their jobs when exposed,' Perdy said vehemently, sounding like Rocco.

'What are you working on, at the moment?'

'I'm researching dog theft, it's on the increase.'

'I didn't think that would be your sort of story.'

'Dognappers threatened to stab the landlord of my local pub,' Perdy said pointedly.

'Vicious,' Tom acknowledged. 'I hear you were studying medicine, what brought you into journalism?'

Perdy pictured her broken self-clinging to Rocco's lifeless body on top of Overlook Mountain. 'A dear friend inspired me to be a reporter,' she said in a trembling voice.

'A group of us are going for a drink after work, fancy coming along?'

'I've got plans for tonight but thanks for the invite.'

'Another time maybe,' Tom said, looking at her intently.

Aware of the tears welling up in her eyes, Perdy was relieved when her heedful boss walked away. Riding a wave of sadness, she placed her front page feature next to Rocco's photograph. Against the frame, the white flower of the peace lily reached upwards like a candle flame. 'The women's story has been told, Rocco,' Perdy said under her breath.

A pinging sound from her computer signalled the stream of emails flooding her inbox. Reading the kind messages from journalists endorsing her work, lifted her spirits: 'Great exposé, the Kenyan government should be shamed into action.'

'I'm working on a piece about trafficked children in the UK, it might interest you.'

Perdy stared at the screen, unable to assimilate the words. 'Back off, you snooping bitch. Get back to the kitchen where you belong.' *What a Neanderthal, writing such boneheaded crap*, she thought.

About to shut down her computer, she noticed her mum's email: 'We're very proud of you sweetheart. Any nice men in the newsroom?'

'For goodness' sake, I've got serious work to do,' Perdy typed in response.

Rereading the vitriolic email, *Back off from what?* she questioned – *child trafficking in Kenya, dognapping in London?*

Perdy looked at her notes about pedigree dogs being stolen from a kennel – 'thieves broke through metal bars, disabling tight security systems.' *Serious crime but nothing like the Lady Gaga story where her dog walker got shot in the chest. No, the hate mail must relate to the trafficking feature.*

'What do you think bonny lad?' she asked Rocco as she gazed at his photograph.

'The bloke's a moron, don't let him rain on your parade,' he said heartily.

"Those whom the Gods love die young", is utter balderdash, Perdy told herself as she sat on the bed drinking cocoa. *Premature death holds no glory, it's just an agonising waste of life.*

In the flat opposite, the glow from the streetlight lamp illuminated a heavily pregnant woman knitting a blanket. Perdy reached out and touched the wing of the eagle, sculpted by her birth mother.

Running her fingers along the serrated edges of the feathers, she was back in the forest with Rocco: '*To Native Americans, golden eagles represent strength and courage,*' she heard him say.

'Thanks to you Rocco, I found my raison d'être in Kenya,' Perdy whispered.

To mark the anniversary of his death, she opened the notebook which recorded her landmark visit to Africa.

Oh, Rocco, it's so much worse than I imagined, talking to the women and hearing their desperate stories, Perdy read. *They have no one to protect them, speak up for them, give them the help they need. It's such a cruel lottery where you are born. In my home city of Newcastle, the aim is to end rough sleeping completely. It's not a utopian dream, there's mental health support, dedicated housing, and education opportunities for vulnerable people. In Nairobi, an estimated 60,000 children live on the streets in appalling conditions. I've seen them in rows, snuggling into their mothers on flimsy strips of cardboard.*

You were right about the scale of baby thefts Rocco, organised cartels traffic children for huge sums of money. The defenceless street mothers are afraid to go to sleep in case their infants get stolen. 'I can't take a nap in the park,' Yara told me, 'someone might steal my baby.'

Maya remembered the exact day and hour her daughter went missing. 'Even though I'm living on the streets, they shouldn't take my child,' she said, in floods of tears. 'Just because I'm homeless doesn't mean I'm a bad mother.' The women's love for their babies is palpable, the traffickers are tearing their hearts apart.

Sasha looked like a child herself, with spikey dreadlocks poking out of her turban and a mud cloth around her shoulders. 'I've looked for my baby everywhere,' she said. 'It feels dreadful not having him with me, he was my whole life.'

Today, I visited an illegal backstreet clinic where women are coerced into selling their babies. 'I have no choice,' Hibbo said, 'it's for the best.' The manipulative midwife had arranged to sell her son for 50,000 dollars to a childless couple.

I also met an undercover reporter who bought a baby from a venal hospital worker. Just as you said Rocco, the street mothers have no status, the authorities turn a blind eye to their suffering. There's so much to write about, these helpless women deserve to be seen and heard.[2]

The final sentence penned in Rocco's words, elicited a maelstrom of emotions for Perdy. She closed her tear-stained notebook and touched the lead feathers of the sculpted eagle. Imagining they were Rocco's extended fingers as he fell to the ground, she clasped them tightly. *Death has not ravaged him, he's holding my hand, guiding me through the forest of life,* Perdy assured herself.

[2] BBC Africa, *The Baby Stealers*, online 2020.

Chapter 8

Perdy stood at the bus stop, reading the church poster, 'There's enough for every man's need but not every man's greed.'[3] Hit by the truth of the words, *I'll increase my charity donations now I'm earning decent money*, she said to herself.

Aware of the air pollution from the traffic, Perdy stepped back from the road and wrapped her African scarf around her mouth. On autopilot like her fellow early-morning commuters, she looked repeatedly for the overdue bus. At the sight of Dick coming round the corner, red-faced and breathless, her heart sank. Using his ample body, he would shunt her into a corner and talk incessantly for the entire journey.

When the doors opened, Perdy rushed onto the bus and sat beside a woman brushing her hair. 'Oh, no, it's starting to rain, I'm going to get drenched,' her neighbour moaned.

Since returning from Kenya where the street women had their babies stolen, these things didn't matter to Perdy anymore. 'I think it's only a shower,' she said.

Seeing the bump under her neighbour's taut coat, Perdy realised she was the blanket-knitting woman from the flat

---

[3] Mahatma Gandhi quotation.

opposite. Reminded of the pitiful Kenyan mothers, she took out the newspaper splashing her front page feature.

'Upsetting story,' the woman said, 'imagine getting your baby stolen.'

'Hopefully, the press coverage will prompt the government to intervene.'

The woman peered at the photo on the masthead of the newspaper. 'Are you the journalist who wrote the article?' she asked.

'I am,' Perdy said. 'I've only recently moved into the area; it feels strange after Africa.'

'I admire your bravery; it takes guts going out there. I work in House of Fraser but I'm about to start maternity leave.'

'When's the baby due?' Perdy asked in a friendly manner.

'Mid-May, thank God, I feel like I've been pregnant forever. Maybe we could meet for coffee sometime, I'll give you the lowdown on the locals.'

The offer took Perdy by surprise, the idea of sitting down and making small talk with a relative stranger horrified her. *You don't have the time, you need to make your mark in a competitive industry,* an inner voice snapped.

The woman looked at her expectantly, waiting for an answer.

'I'd love to go for a coffee,' Perdy forced herself to say.

'Great, I don't usually catch the bus so I'll give you my mobile number.'

My counsellor will be thrilled I've got something to talk about other than my job and Rocco's death, Perdy thought as she made a note of Jeannie's details. She was pleased it had stopped raining by the time her newfound friend alighted from the bus. *It isn't only French women who want to look their best,* Perdy happily acknowledged.

Afraid of windbag Dick pouncing down next to her, she stayed strategically in the aisle seat. Thinking of work, she ignored her mum's WhatsApp message of the day and googled child trafficking in the UK. Having surmised that the victims were mainly from Romania, Vietnam and such places, Perdy was surprised to learn that more than a quarter of children trafficked in the UK were British. Through a grubby window, she looked piercingly at the streets as if she were seeing them for the first time.

In the open-plan office, Perdy found a free workstation in the middle of the room and logged in. Energised by the cacophony of ringing phones and multiple conversations, she glanced over at Tom. In his garish checked shirt, he looked like a lumberjack, chopping down a forest of words.

He switched off his computer and strode over to Perdy's desk with a gleam in his eye. 'Terrific news,' he said, 'the Kenyan police have arrested hospital staff in connection with the stolen babies.'

'About time too. It should have happened a long time ago,' Perdy said triumphantly.

'The government have released a statement saying it would do its utmost to root out widespread human trafficking. I know the BBC covered this story but your freelance feature added weight to the exposé.'

'I simply talked to the women who wanted their stories told, they highlighted the scale of the problem.'

'Yes, but you did it off your own back – showed initiative, a natural born hack.'

'Not quite, I had a few false starts before I found my calling.'

'Here's something which will interest you,' Tom said, handing her a photograph. 'Ryan's had his dog stolen – not unusual I know, but he has selective mutism.'

Perdy saw the bliss in the young boy's eyes as he cuddled his curly-haired spaniel. 'I'd love to cover the story,' she said.

'Thanks, Perdy, it's got a strong human interest angle. You missed a great night out by the way, we went to a comedy club. Joe got up and ranted on about his divorce. "Ever likely she left you mate – you're a boring bastard," someone shouted out.'

'Sounds like fun,' Perdy said, regretful she'd lost the confidence to have a good time.

'You should have the link to the dognapping story. I'll be in the pub after work if you want to discuss it.'

Somewhere along the line, like an upside-down carriage with wheels in the air, I've derailed from normality. I need to push myself to get back on track, back on track, Perdy told herself, as Tom walked away.

Having encountered it in her medical training, Perdy had a genuine interest in selective mutism. *Some of the children talk freely to their families but are speechless outside the house*, she recalled.

'Let's find the spaniel, Rocco,' Perdy said, moving his photograph into the pool of sunlight hitting her desk.

Chapter 9

Overriding the anxiety making her heart race, Perdy searched for Tom in the crowded pub. A bloke in a Mr Right t-shirt, accidentally knocked into her as he staggered to the toilet. His mate, pretending to be a Good Samaritan, pressed against her like a crushing barrier. Taking control, she ground her boot heel hard into his canvas shoe and made her escape.

About to exit, Perdy noticed a snug decked-out with theatre posters at the far side of the bar. *A wood-panelled sanctuary away from the mayhem, Tom's sort of place*, she thought as she stepped towards the room.

When Joe saw her, he moved his crumpled Mac from the seat next to him and waved.

'Great, you've made it,' Tom said enthusiastically as if she'd passed some initiation test. 'Joe's going to the bar, what do you want to drink?'

'A pineapple juice,' Perdy replied, waiting for some witty banter at her expense.

'Sensible,' Tom said, rolling up his sleeves, 'too many journalists have a drink problem.'

Given his lean body and steady temperament, Perdy guessed he was a man of moderation.

'Thanks for setting me up with the dognapping story,' she said, taking the seat next to Joe's.

'Visit Ryan, hear what he's got to say,' Tom suggested.

'He's too anxious to speak to strangers,' Perdy said, 'that's the root of selective mutism.'

'It's not all about words. Get him to do some drawings, he'll be desperate to communicate.'

'I spoke to his mother, she's grateful for the press coverage.'

'Your feature could prompt an important lead,' Tom said.

'Ryan thinks it's his fault the dog's been stolen. He was playing with the spaniel in the garden but when a bloke started talking to him, he bolted into the house. By the time he returned to the garden, Willow had disappeared.'

'Poor kid, he must have been traumatised.'

'Still is,' Perdy said, 'he looks for the dog everywhere.'

In the natural silence that settled between them, she visualised Ryan searching in vain for his stolen spaniel.

'Fancy coming to the comedy club?' Tom asked. 'Joe wants to try out some new divorce jokes.'

'I'm not in the mood for fun and laughter,' Perdy said, 'I've been receiving misogynistic emails.'

'Just spineless trolls jealous of your talent. Block the bastards.'

'Wish I could, it's like fighting the hate squad.'

'These men don't like having successful women around.'

'They'd better get used to it, we're here to stay.'

'That's the spirit, let me know how it goes with Ryan and the family. There might be an opportunity to cover selective mutism.'

'It's certainly something a lot of people don't understand.'

'Imagine being terrified to speak outside the home.'

'And losing your pet dog as a consequence.'

'Heartbreaking,' Tom said as Joe put the drinks down on the table.

Tom's drawing idea was a non-starter. In Perdy's presence, whatever Ryan was thinking was locked firmly in his head. Cocooned in silence, the flaxen-haired boy pulled up the hood on his sweater and turned to the wall. Tensing his body and clenching his fists, he froze like an impenetrable statue.

His mother gazed at her fretful son, her love and concern reflecting in her sky-blue eyes. 'Talk to him,' she whispered, 'tell him why you're here.'

Perdy moved closer to the boy and stooped down to his level. 'Hello Ryan, I'm going to write a story for the newspaper about your missing dog,' she said warmly.

'It might help get Willow back sweetheart,' his mother added.

As if they had been waiting for the right moment to enter, Ryan's father and sister stepped into the room. Seeing her distressed brother, the little girl ran to his side and wrapped her arms around him. 'Willow will be home soon,' she said soothingly like a much older child.

Through the open doorway, Perdy could see the dog's leather collar hanging over the banister.

'Thanks for coming, we've all been looking forward to your visit,' the father said, radiating positivity. 'Ryan told us the dognapper was wearing a brown jacket and look what I found on the lawn.'

In his hand lay a chunky bronze button on pure white paper. 'A gift from the gods,' he added in an upbeat voice.

Ryan turned from the wall and stepped nervously behind his sister, a small human shield. Although his eyes shone with curiosity, his lips stayed firmly shut, clamping him in silence. Perdy recalled the fear of speaking her mind until Rocco came into her life.

'Can I take a photograph of the button?' she asked, taking out her camera.

'A good idea, it's pretty distinctive,' the father said.

No one drew attention to Ryan scuttling around the periphery of the room into the kitchen. Instead, the family looked on as Perdy focused her lens on the notable find.

Perdy viewed the tranquil garden with rising vexation: '*What kind of person steals the dog of a vulnerable child?*' she questioned.

The sound of Ryan nattering freely inside the house lifted her spirits.

'It took us a long time to realise my son had selective mutism,' his father said, 'he's such a chatterbox at home.'

'Is it alright if I mention his disability in my feature?' Perdy asked. 'It might shame someone into returning the dog.'

'Go ahead, it's a chance to highlight selective mutism. Many people think Ryan is choosing not to talk when in fact, he's too terrified to speak to strangers.'

'Your daughter's remarkable with him,' Perdy said.

'She is. They both adore Willow, he's the rock and soul of the family.'

Perdy wrote down the heartfelt words and closed her notebook. 'Thanks for your time,' she said, 'I'll do my best to trace the heinous thief.'

Perdy began to write the feature in her head as she walked towards her flat. No need to embellish the story, the hard-hitting facts would speak for themselves: *170 per cent increase in dognapping; organised criminals creating human misery.*

Rooting around for her key, she recoiled at the layers of disintegrated tissue lining her bag. Relieved to feel its sharp edges in her hand, she looked up to see Dick leering at her from across the road. Already unnerved by the stream of misogynistic emails, his fixated stare made her shudder. *Has he been waiting for me, or is he prowling the vicinity watching all single women?* Perdy asked herself.

Anxious to escape the lingering creep, twice she misaligned her key in the lock. Dick's presence loomed over her like a ghoulish shadow. She cleared her head and with doctor-like precision, inserted the chiselled metal into the door. Hurrying inside, she threw down her bag and with two hands slammed it shut. 'Sod off, you pervert,' she yelled, kicking the tacky junk mail piled in the hallway.

Chapter 10

To the sharp sound of a Spanish guitar, Perdy arched her arms above her head like a flamenco dancer. Transported by the music, she imagined the dressing gown flapping around her legs was a vibrant gypsy dress. She moved around the room stomping her feet until the ring of the doorbell rooted her to the spot.

Not expecting any deliveries, Perdy feared that creepy Dick was standing in her porchway. When the bell rang a second time, she turned off the music and peered through a chink in the curtains.

Jeannie with her rich auburn hair was looking up at the flat anticipating signs of life. Perdy got dressed quickly and raced down the stairs to greet her welcome visitor.

'Sorry if I'm a tad early,' Jeannie said, 'I'm finding it difficult to sleep, at the moment. I've baked this cake for you, a welcome to the neighbourhood present.'

Perdy looked at the fuchsia pink icing and smiled. 'It's gorgeous,' she said, 'thank you.'

Unused to spontaneous acts of friendship, she hesitated before inviting Jeannie into her sparsely decorated flat. 'Do you want to come in?' she asked tentatively.

'I'm going into town to buy some baby things. Fancy meeting up for that coffee later?'

'That'll be great, text me a time and place and I'll be there.'

'People round here will welcome you with open arms,' Jeannie said, 'they're a friendly bunch.'

Knowing herself to be a private person at heart, Perdy recoiled at the idea of being submerged in a community.

'Enjoy the cake,' Jeannie said, making Perdy smile even though her stomach was churning.

Whilst she was waving goodbye to her amicable neighbour, Perdy noticed a young girl in a beanie hat dodging the traffic. Safe on the pavement, the child stood under a pine tree and reached into the pocket of her dungarees. Clutching a small packet tightly in her fist, the girl froze like a timid fawn.

A ghoulish-looking youth in saggy trousers exited from Jeannie's block of flats and strolled towards her. He glanced furtively around before hovering over the child to block her from view.

Perdy placed the cake in the porch and stepped forward on the pretext of moving the bin. She watched the bloke shuffle back to his lair with his head down. The girl took a second package from her pocket and this time slid it behind her back. She positioned herself rigidly in the same place under the tree, as if carrying out instructions.

A woman pulled up in a Mini Cooper and beckoned the deadpan child over to her vehicle. Through an open window, the girl delivered the clandestine packet with her tiny hand. Without engaging with the recipient, she pulled down her beanie hat and hurried away.

Perdy crossed the road to follow her but the girl bounded around a corner, out of view. Side-stepping a lady using a pooper scooper, Perdy sprinted after her into a dingy back street. In the distance, she caught sight of the girl's beautiful red hair as she jumped into a transit van. Perdy groaned as it sped away. *A child coerced into drug dealing in broad daylight, what sort of area am I living in?* she asked herself.

Relieved to be back in her flat, Perdy ignored her ringing phone until she'd filled the kettle. Realising the unexpected call was from her mother, she dialled home in a panicky frame of mind: 'Hi Mum, is everything alright?' she asked.

'More than alright,' her mum said, 'I'm throwing a party.'

'You're not normally so sociable, what's the special occasion?'

'A community get-together, there's someone I'd like you to meet.'

'If you're trying to matchmake, forget it. I don't want a boyfriend.'

'A fortnight today, 8.00 pm, our house. Trust me, you'll have a fabulous time.'

I don't have a fabulous time these days, Perdy wanted to say.

'Stan sent a letter by the way, he's coming over in the autumn,' her mother said.

'Really? That's a surprise.'

'That's what I thought, perhaps he wants to see someone in particular.'

The innuendo in her mother's voice made Perdy cringe.

'I've got to go, Mum,' she said, 'I want to make a start on my feature before meeting Jeannie.'

'I look forward to seeing you soon sweetheart. Bye.'

Perdy tugged at her hair as she often did in times of stress. Stan's visit would unleash a torrent of memories of her fateful summer. She recalled riding in his boat on the glistening lake before Rocco's death flung her into troubled waters. A fresh wave of pain, carrying fragments of the past washed over her. She let it ebb away and reached for her cherry blossom mug to lighten her mood.

A surge of people in red and white football shirts came towards Perdy as she walked to the cafe. The devoted fans of a struggling team moved in harmony as if being called to prayer. To avoid them, she cut through the park and past the awkward teens straddling the kiddies' swings up to the lawn.

Much to the delight of his family, a young boy threw a ball for his cockapoo to chase. Perdy knew dognappers were hardened criminals but she hoped her feature would help find Ryan's spaniel. A trained journalist, her mind raced to her next story: *Children coerced into selling drugs for thuggish gangs; ruthless villainy ruining young lives.*

To dissipate her anger, she perused the mass of rhododendrons rambling around a tree. Sensing someone behind her, she turned to see Dick with his bristly face admiring the flowers.

'They're beautiful aren't they,' he said, edging closer to her.

'I've got to meet a friend for a coffee,' Perdy blurted out as she stepped away.

'Have a nice time,' he said, giving her a lingering look.

Pleased to be wearing her trainers, Perdy hastened up the path towards the cat cafe to meet Jeannie.

She saw her cake-making friend huddled in a corner with a smile on her face.

'Nice choice of venue,' Perdy said. 'How did you know I'm a cat person?'

'I didn't,' Jeannie answered, 'but I can use my gourmet card in here.'

'Every penny counts,' Perdy said, catching sight of all the shopping piled on the floor.

'Expensive things babies, they take up all your money.'

And your time and energy, Perdy thought, wondering if she would ever be in the right head space to become a mother.

'Do you like this?' Jeannie said, producing a brown onesie with 'locally brewed' on the front.

'Different,' Perdy said with a laugh. An exquisitely marked tortoiseshell cat padded towards her, making her feel at home.

'How have you settled in?' Jeannie asked, handing her a menu.

Perdy decided to be honest. 'The flat's great or will be once I get it sorted but I think Dick's stalking me.'

Jeannie put down her menu. 'He's watching over you,' she said softly, 'making sure you don't come to any harm.'

'Really!' Perdy exclaimed. 'He's not my father.'

'His daughter was murdered by a stalker last year. Dick patrols the streets keeping an eye open for single women.'

Perdy was stunned. 'Guess I'm just getting to know people in the area,' she said. 'What a devastation for Dick's family.'

'It was a shocking event; this is a relatively crime-free area.'

Perdy resisted the temptation to mention the child she'd seen earlier in the day peddling drugs.

'Are you getting anything to eat?' she asked.

'I am,' Jeannie said. 'Two tea cakes with extra butter.'

Perdy looked out of the window, *a welcoming community for some, a living hell for others.*

Chapter 11

Perdy waited for Jeannie to go to the toilet before reading the press coverage of the murder. Dick's only child had been killed on a gloomy towpath by a persistent stalker. He stated that on five separate occasions, male police officers had belittled his daughter's pleas for help. *Bastard misogynists, silencing the voice of a pitiful woman*, Perdy thought to herself.

Jeannie called over from the counter, 'Just getting a smoothie, can I get you anything?'

Perdy shook her head and stroked a fat tabby purring on the windowsill. She admired the cat's contentment, her own bullying inner voice made her life stressful. *Don't forget you've got that feature to write*, it taunted.

Perdy looked at Jeannie's raspberry smoothie being placed on the table. 'You know, I might just get one of those,' she said.

The lad with the pompadour hair, clearing the table, nodded approvingly. 'Good choice, they're delicious. I'll bring one over for you.'

'Nice to see someone enjoying their job,' Jeannie remarked. 'We used to be like that at House of Fraser but everyone's afraid of closure these days.'

'Regional press is the same. There's no job security, that's why I'm working for the Nationals.'

'Good for you, you're a talented journalist. Have you got any big stories in the pipeline?'

'I'm working on a feature about dognapping.'

'Serious stuff, totally different to catnapping,' Jeannie said, with reference to the sleeping moggies sprawled on the floor.

Perdy's face brightened. 'There's something you might be able to help me with,' she said.

Keen to assist, Jeannie leaned forward with an attentive expression on her face.

Perdy showed her a photo of the chunky brown button found in Ryan's garden. 'We're pretty sure this came from the thief's coat. Do you recognise the brand?'

'That's come from a Lyle and Scott jacket, we sell them in the store. In fact, I sold one last month to a man with a star tattoo on his neck.'

Perdy re-examined the button in the photo. 'It's brand new,' she stated.

'The bloke lives in Brickfields near my nan. He's got a cute boy who loves her whippet.'

'Give me his address, I'll snoop around, see if he's acquired a dog of his own.'

'He doesn't look like the sort to be a dognapper but it's an interesting lead. House Of Fraser's a popular store for menswear.'

Perdy imagined Jeannie floating out of a bottle to bring her luck. 'Things don't run smoothly for me,' she said, 'but it's worth a shot.'

Brickfields surprised Perdy, she'd visualised a soulless, concrete jungle with mean-looking, high-rise flats. Instead, it was a smart neighbourhood decked with trees and architecturally designed houses. Perdy reimagined the man with the star tattoo as a hard-working creative who valued decorative body art. *Why would he steal a dog?* she wondered.

A woman pushing a miniature dachshund in a pram stopped to make it more comfortable. 'He's had surgery,' she explained, 'this is his first ride out.'

'I hope he gets better soon,' Perdy said, scanning the street.

'Can I help you with anything?' the woman asked.

'I'm looking for my friend's house. He's got a tricoloured spaniel; you might know him.'

'Oh yes, I do,' she replied. 'Jack bought the dog for his son's birthday, the boy was thrilled. They live over there in the house with the blue shutters.'

'Thanks so much,' Perdy said, eyeing the number on the wrought iron gate. Her spirits lifted: *131 Lime Avenue, the same address supplied by Jeannie's nan.* Aware that she might have located the dognapper, she hovered in the street hoping to catch a glimpse of the spaniel.

A boy, about the same age as Ryan, ran into the garden. 'Berty,' he cried out, 'fetch your ball.'

A black and white dog came briefly to the doorway before skulking back into the house. Perdy's heart sank; *not a tricoloured coloured spaniel after all.* About to retrace her steps, she caught sight of a man in a brown jacket stepping onto the lawn.

'Come on Berty, see what Daddy's got,' he called to the dog crouching in the window.

Enticed by the offering, the spaniel re-emerged and crept towards the treats cupped in the man's hands. Visible brown markings on the side of its silky coat piqued Perdy's interest. The dog turned its head to the biscuits, revealing the copper-tanned patches above its eyes. *Ryan's pet in a new family home.* 'Willow, Willow,' Perdy hollered, to attract the spaniel's attention.

The man sprang towards her like a soldier in combat. 'The dog's called Berty,' he snapped, 'sod off.'

'You've stolen the spaniel from a boy who has selective mutism,' Perdy said.

'Absolute rubbish,' the man retorted. 'You're mad.'

'Either you return the dog or I report you to the police.'

'Interfering busybody, what's it got to do with you?' the man snarled.

'I'm a journalist covering the story,' Perdy said, 'is there anything you want to tell me?'

The man started to tremble. 'I can't talk here,' he said, 'meet me in the park in ten minutes.'

'What possessed you to steal from a child?' Perdy asked.

'Desperation,' the man said tearfully. 'I wish I'd never done it.'

In the park, Perdy read the words on a memorial bench: 'Those we love, don't go away.' *Too true*, she thought, drawing strength from Rocco's abiding presence. 'This dognapping scenario doesn't make sense,' she told him. 'It's more complicated than I thought.'

'Nothing's ever black and white,' he said, 'unless it's a Newcastle United football scarf.'

Before she could reply, Perdy saw the man in the brown jacket striding towards her.

Up close, with his purplish eyes and fretful expression, he looked on the verge of a nervous breakdown.

'I'll come clean,' the man said, 'provided my boy can keep the spaniel for one more night.'

Perdy balked at the absurdity of the request. 'Dognapping's a heinous crime, the family need their dog back.'

'I know,' the man said struggling for breath. 'I've done something incredibly wrong, something I didn't mean to do.'

His harrowed face twitched with anxiety as he collapsed onto the bench. Aware of his agitation, Perdy sat down beside him to hear his confession.

'My wife gave me the money to buy Teddy a dog for his birthday and I gambled it away,' he said.

Perdy edged closer to him to signify her willingness to listen.

'When the boy ran into the house, in a moment of complete madness, I took the spaniel for my son.'

'Does your wife know the dog's stolen?' Perdy asked.

'No, I couldn't tell her. She thinks I've got the gambling under control.'

'Tell her everything,' Perdy advised. 'Give her the chance to support you.'

'I hate myself. Who steals a dog from a helpless child?'

'You'll hate yourself even more if you don't return the spaniel.'

'I can't believe I've told you all this.'

'You needed to tell someone.'

The man looked at her earnestly. 'My son will be distraught but I'll do the right thing.'

A bittersweet situation, Perdy thought, *happiness for Ryan but bewildering pain for another little boy.*

Chapter 12

Oblivious of the time, Perdy sat in her flat knitting a matinee jacket for Jeannie's baby. To erase a feeling of dread about the dognapper, she focused on the rhythmic clicking of the needles. *What if he can't find the strength to tell his wife and looks for a way out?* she asked herself.

The noise of a vehicle screeching to a halt in the street amplified her jitters. She stopped stitching and stared into the blackness of the night. A new shoot from her cheese plant furled against the window like a miniature spear. Despite being weary, she strolled across the room to examine the fresh leaf.

Under the glow of a streetlamp, Perdy saw a grey transit van parked outside the greengrocers. Six boys in fashionable clothes sprang from the vehicle in quick succession. Perdy watched a thickset bloke pat each of them on the back as they made their way into the shop. *Not a football coach pleased with his players*, she thought, *more like a drug trafficker exploiting children.*

'Give that overactive mind a rest and get to bed,' Rocco said.

'Hold on,' she told him. 'A young girl's appeared from the shadows and is shouting at the bloke. Oh my God, he's smacked her across the face and is shoving her into the road.'

Charged with adrenaline, Perdy grabbed her coat and ran down the stairs to intervene. By the time she arrived on the scene, the bloke had retreated into the shop and the girl was slumped on the pavement.

Perdy stooped down next to the shaken teenager. 'Are you alright?' she asked caringly.

'My brother's in there,' the girl said, pointing to the greengrocers, 'and they won't let me see him.'

'Is he with friends?'

'He thinks he is, but he's in real danger!' the girl exclaimed. 'Kevin's vicious, he beat up my boyfriend for no reason.'

'For no reason?' Perdy queried.

The teenager bristled with rage. 'Jamie wanted to break free from that bastard but Kevin said he owed him money for food and rent.'

'Have you been to the police?'

'My brother would kill me if I did, he thinks he's got the job of his dreams working for Kevin.'

'And has he?' Perdy asked, hoping she would say more.

'No, he's caught up in a fucking nightmare. We wouldn't be in this position if mam were still alive.'

The girl's raw pain emanating from her body struck Perdy hard. 'Do you live around here?' she asked.

'I've moved into Green Lees children's home, it's less than a mile away.'

'You're shivering, do you fancy a coffee?'

'Thanks, but I've got to get back. I've got some homework I want to finish.'

'Good for you,' Perdy said, impressed by her attitude.

'Frank's thrown the towel in at school but I'm working hard for mam's sake. Kevin's not destroying our entire family.'

The girl jumped up and straightened her skirt. 'I might see you again sometime,' she said, 'I'll be keeping my eye on that greengrocers.'

'And so will I,' Perdy called out as the teenager fled into the starless night.

I'm lucky to have my overattentive mum, Perdy thought as she put the knitting away in a drawer. *I wonder who she's lined up for me at the party? No doubt some dowdy jobsworth who doesn't do sexy moves on the dance floor.* Perdy managed to smile about the ludicrous situation, despite the veracity of her hunch.

On the verge of drawing her bedroom curtains, she looked out at the unobtrusive exterior of the greengrocers.

'There's more being sold over there than cabbages and carrots,' she told Rocco. 'Those boys are being used to traffic drugs.'

'Get to bed, you've done enough for today,' he said.

Reflecting on the night's events, Perdy plumped up her pillow more aggressively than she intended. 'We're coming to get you Kevin,' she said vehemently. 'You and all the other monsters ruining young lives.'

Too exhausted to make a supper drink, Perdy lay down on her bed and closed her eyes. Steering her mind to something joyful, she pictured the long-eared spaniel licking Ryan's ecstatic face.

Later, in the golden glow of dawn, she succumbed to an unruly nightmare; the spaniel metamorphosed into a mewling baby wrapped in a pink blanket. Perdy's mother lifted the newborn from her crib and showered her with kisses. Fayola wailed piteously for her lost daughter until a slamming door muted her voice.

The loud roar of a car engine starting up outside woke Perdy with a start. Hot and clammy from the vividness of her dream, she remembered the imperilled boys across the road. To mollify her fear, she placed her hand firmly over the sculpted eagle by the side of her bed. '*Stay bold and brave my English rose*,' she heard Fayola say. '*Use your talent, make your mark*.'

Chapter 13

On the bus, despite the empty window seats, Perdy chose to sit next to Dick.

His face beamed when he saw her. 'Good news about Jeannie,' he said.

'What do you mean?' Perdy asked keenly.

'She had a baby boy in the early hours of the morning. Stanley Joey Jordan according to his dad.'

'That's wonderful,' Perdy said with a sudden burst of joy.

'Billy says he'd settled down to watch Top Gear when Jeannie went into labour.'

'It must have taken them by surprise, she wasn't even on maternity leave.'

'It was the best day of my life when Emma was born.'

'I was sorry to hear about your daughter's awful death.'

'Thank you,' Dick said, falling uncharacteristically silent.

Understanding his need for private thought, Perdy took out her phone to check her work emails. 'Fantastic,' she muttered when she read Tom's message.

'Everything alright?' Dick asked.

'Yes,' Perdy said, embarrassed by her indiscretion. 'A stolen spaniel's been returned to its owners.'

'You work at The Gazette, don't you? The paper did a good job covering Emma's murder.'

'I read the reports, shocking negligence by the police.'

'They repeatedly ignored my beautiful girl.'

'Scandalous, they should have been sacked.'

'I was eaten with rage but all those people attending Emma's vigil gave me strength.'

'It takes courage to keep on going,' Perdy said, lightly touching Dick's arm.

'It makes no sense to give in, we need to make things safer for women. There's going to be a Reclaim the Streets march next month.'

'I'll definitely be there,' Perdy said, wanting to show solidarity.

'I'd be lost without the support of the community, the folk around here have been amazing.'

Perdy remembered the boys hidden among the cabbages on the rotten side of the street. 'There's good and bad everywhere,' she said.

Eager to get into work early, Perdy raced past a group of coffee-sipping commuters blocking the pavement. A labourer with a dirty face, wolf-whistled her from a dugout hole in the road. Without flinching, she strode past the man-child with her head held high. *What a momentous day*, Perdy thought as she neared the newspaper office, *Jeannie's had her baby and the spaniel's been returned.*

Ferreting around in her bag for her staff pass, she noticed a woman in a trouser suit standing outside Thornton House.

When the stranger saw Perdy, she walked purposefully towards her as if they had prearranged a meeting.

'Can I have a word?' she asked, unable to hide the desperation in her voice.

'If it's anything to do with a news story, let's go into the office,' Perdy said.

The woman stayed still. 'You probably saved my husband's life, Jack was in an extremely dark place when he spoke to you yesterday. Thanks for listening to him.'

'I take it he told you everything.'

'He did eventually. Gambling cuts you off from those closest to you.'

'What did you tell your little boy?'

'That Daddy had found the lost spaniel wandering the streets and that he belonged to another family.'

'How did he take it?'

'Teddy was heartbroken but we promised we'd get him another dog.'

'How's your husband?' Perdy asked, feeling empathy for the family.

'No one likes lying to his own son but he couldn't tell Teddy the truth. Jack did well to tell me that he'd stolen the spaniel. What will you write in your feature?'

Good question, Perdy thought grasping the reason for their encounter.

'I certainly won't be writing any lies,' Perdy said, 'but it's the call of my news editor how much of the story we tell.'

'If the whole truth comes out, it will push Jack over the edge,' the woman said emotionally.

'I'll do my best but I can't make any promises. Ryan being reunited with his spaniel will make a great feature but I don't make the call.'

'Jack said you were a good person. I hope to God things work out.'

Perdy found herself wringing her hands as she watched the woman walk down the street. *I might be asked to write a feature which could ruin someone's life,* she realised with a queasy feeling of dread. The shine taken off her day, she leapt up the steps to Thornton House to battle on Jack's behalf.

From her desk, Perdy could see Tom's earnest face as he prepared the daily news briefing. *He's a top-notch journalist,* she thought, *if Tom knows the whole story, he'll want to print it.*

The woman's voice rang in her ears*: 'If the truth comes out, it will push Jack over the edge.'*

To stop herself from being wrenched in two, Perdy gazed at Rocco's photograph beside the Peace Lily. Touching the tip of the white flower, she waited for his wise words to steady her through the storm. 'You've proved you're a strong lady, trust your gut,' Rocco said.

With a plan in mind, Perdy walked towards the news desk with a smile on her face.

'Morning Tom, wonderful news about the spaniel.'

'Hi Perdy, I thought you'd be pleased. Apparently, Ryan shouted from his bedroom in the early hours of the morning that Willow was back home. His parents thought he was dreaming until they heard the dog barking in the garden.'

'Do the family know who returned the dog?'

'By the time Simon got downstairs, there was no one in sight. It's a sick person who steals a dog from a child, I guess someone's conscience kicked in.'

Hit by the aptness of his words, Perdy tried to steer the conversation away from the dognapper's identity. 'I'm delighted for Ryan, do you want me to visit the family?' she asked brightly.

'The dad's a keen photographer, he's already sent us some great photos. Just talk to him on the phone, I need your help with a breaking story.'

An oppressive weight lifted from Perdy's shoulders. Thanks to a busy news day, Jack had slipped from the noose.

'A pity you didn't get a lead on the brown button, finding the dognapper would have strengthened the piece.'

Telling no lies, Perdy grasped the moment. 'What's the breaking story?' she asked in a professional tone.

'Kids going missing from a local children's home. We've got a tip-off that someone's using them to traffic drugs.'

'Have they disappeared from Green Lees?' Perdy asked, thinking of the girl searching for her brother.

'No, Shotley Park. A care worker rang to say the police have been laissez-faire about the boys' disappearance.'

'The "I don't give a shit" squad.'

'It takes a good journalist like you to hunt out the truth.'

Perdy blushed at Tom's unexpected praise. 'Let's get the real story out there,' she said, 'someone knows what's happened to those boys.'

Chapter 14

The care worker with her blonde hair and stylish clothes looked like a Swedish au pair.

'Boys are going missing and the police couldn't care less,' she said, getting straight to the point.

'What makes you think they're being used to traffic drugs?' Perdy asked.

'One of the girls overheard them bragging about their business phones.'

'When did she tell you this?'

'Two days ago. Tina came into my office fuming because Tommy had missed his birthday tea. She said it was unfair that he'd gone on a job when she'd baked a Thomas the Tank Engine cake for him.'

'Did Tina say what Tommy's job entailed?'

'No, but she mentioned he had multiple phones.'

'Sounds ominous. Have you mentioned this to the police?'

'Not yet. I want some evidence that the boys were groomed.'

'Who could be recruiting the boys to peddle drugs?'

'I haven't a clue. The staff here are incredible, they go that extra mile to give the kids hope for the future.'

Perdy smiled but her sharp, journalistic mind was taking nothing at face value. 'Why have you involved the press?' she asked.

'Six boys have vanished in the past six months. No one seems bothered because they live in a children's home, I want their lives to matter.'

There must be Police Officers targeting County Line gangs with a vengeance, Perdy thought as she took out her notebook. 'I'm not a detective but this is my kind of story. Does anyone have contact with the kids apart from family members?' she asked.

'Yes, we organise various activities to keep them busy. My boyfriend gives guitar lessons to wannabe musicians, plus a dance teacher and football coach teach unisex classes.'

'What about tradespeople, maintenance workers, those sorts of visitors?'

'The usual, essential workers – a gardener, window cleaner, handy Andy who does the repairs.'

Perdy caught sight of the emerald green lawn flanked by rows of purple allium.

'The gardener does an amazing job,' she said. 'Do any of the children help him?'

'No. They're not drawn to nature; they prefer trawling the back streets.'

'Not everyone. There's a girl with a camera around her neck, sitting under the laburnum tree.'

'Oh, that's Tina. We gave her a camera to distract her from missing Tommy.'

'Was he her boyfriend?'

'It's hard to tell these days. The teenagers change partners like speed dating contestants.'

'But they were close?'

'I would say so, friendships run deep in the home.'

'Do you mind if I have a word with her in private?'

'That's a good idea, she might disclose something new.'

The sound of a guitar being played in the next room made Perdy's heart flutter. For a blissful moment, she thought Rocco was serenading her from his cabin.

'Something on your mind?' Sue asked, bringing her back to the real world.

A sharp pain stabbed at Perdy's chest. 'A memory,' she stammered out.

Perdy waited for the go-ahead before joining Tina under the yellow-chained laburnum tree. Up close, the teenager's tawdry makeup made her look much older than her years. Perdy wanted to tell her she'd look prettier without it but she understood the importance of putting on a face to confront the world.

'Have you taken any good photos?' she asked to kick start the conversation.

'Not yet,' Tina answered. 'I took some selfies but I looked horrendous so I've deleted them.'

Perdy wondered if boys had the same degree of vulnerability about their appearance. 'I've come to talk about Tommy,' she said, knowing this would pique Tina's interest.

'Well, he's a bastard, going off like that.'

'I understand why you're angry but Tommy could be in danger.'

'It's his own fault, he doesn't have to sell drugs,' Tina blurted out.

Perdy spoke caringly like a bosom pal: 'There's a possibility Tommy's been groomed. Do you know what I mean by that?'

'They mentioned something about grooming in school but they were talking about men taking advantage of girls.'

'It's the same thing. Someone acts as a special friend before exploiting their victim.'

'Tommy's not a victim, he earns good money doing his job.'

'What he's doing is illegal, Tina. He could go to jail. Can you think of anyone who plied him with gifts before he went missing?'

The teenager wiggled one foot up and down as she spoke: 'I know who gave him an expensive puffer jacket and a mobile phone.'

'Who is that someone Tina?'

'I won't tell you his name because that would be snitching but I'll give you a clue.'

'Remember, you'll be helping Tommy and all the other missing boys.'

'The bloke's not what he seems.'

'I need a bit more than that Tina.'

'He plays the guitar and he's got a girlfriend who dotes on him.'

The shocking revelation made in such a childlike manner made Perdy feel nauseous. 'That's a big help, Tina,' she said, touching her shoulder. 'I hope you get some fab photos to show Tommy when he returns home.'

To refresh her mind, Perdy watched the bluetits peck at the bird feeder in quick succession. As their heads bobbed up and down, she imagined them being dipped in ink to signify their beauty. Behind them, the pampas grass looked like a feathery backdrop to a stage show.

'Perdy, do you want a coffee?' Sue called out from the porch.

She wished it was Jeannie hailing her for a girly chat, not a doomed woman awaiting her fate. 'I'd prefer a glass of water,' Perdy said with a smile.

The icy cold drink was already on the table when she entered the kitchen.

'How did it go with Tina? Did she divulge anything new?' Sue asked hopefully.

'She told me that someone had given Tommy expensive gifts.'

'That's an amazing breakthrough. I don't suppose she told you who.'

'She inferred it was your boyfriend,' Perdy said in an emotionless voice.

'Tina's lying, Jim can hardly pay his rent let alone afford expensive gifts.'

'Is there any possibility she's telling the truth?'

'None whatsoever. Jim's a caring, gentle soul. That girl has issues.'

'How long have you known your boyfriend for?'

'Six months. I met him on Tinder.'

'Who suggested the guitar lessons, you or him?'

'He did. Jim's generous and kind, he wanted to help the kids in some way.'

'I need you to think carefully, Sue. Did he give lessons to the missing boys?'

'He did but that doesn't mean he's implicated in their disappearance.'

'No, but he might be.'

'Jim's the nicest person I've ever met.'

Perdy decided not to mention all the gruesome murders committed by so-called "beautiful" people. 'When did the first boy go missing?' she asked.

'Six months ago.'

'Was Jim giving him lessons at the time?'

Without answering, Sue ran from the room and shouted for Tina to come in from the garden.

When she returned, she slumped down on a chair like a broken teenager. 'Tina's jealous I've got a boyfriend and she hasn't. Some of these kids are nuts,' she said.

'We can't leave this here,' Perdy told her. 'It's about time we talked to the police.'

'Jim's the best thing that's ever happened to me. I know he's innocent.'

Tina stood in the doorway, glaring defiantly. 'He gave Tommy an expensive puffer jacket and a phone,' she said, cockily.

'Jim's got nothing to do with peddling drugs,' Sue retorted.

'That's for the police to decide. Some men are capable of great deception,' Perdy said.

'Your boyfriend's as guilty as hell,' Tina called out.

Outraged by the comment, Sue leapt up from her chair and ran towards the audacious girl. Perdy jumped between them and grabbed the care worker's hand before it smacked down on Tina's head. Without flinching, the teenager pelted from the stormy scene like an animal escaping danger.

Perdy waited patiently for Sue to stop pacing the room before she spoke again. 'I'm sorry, no one wants to discover their boyfriend's been using them but I believe Tina,' she said. 'The boys could be in danger and there's a suggestion that they've been groomed. We need to let the police know.'

'There were absolutely no warning signs,' Sue said, shifting her viewpoint. 'I feel like I've been violated.'

'Bad blokes don't define who women are. Keep your dignity and take control.'

'Let's go to the police. I want to find out the truth.'

Oh my God, Perdy thought with a rush of dread, *what if the guitarist is operating in a number of children's homes?*

Chapter 15

In Perdy's mind, the men clinging together outside the pub looked like a peculiar beast. Pleased to be sober and in control, she didn't envy their drunken camaraderie. After the day's events, she wanted to talk to like-minded people capable of conversation.

A ravishing ballet poster of "Swan Lake" caught Perdy's attention as she entered the snug. The male dancer with heavily made-up eyes was the antithesis of the beer-swilling men in the street.

'Matthew Bourne's company, my husband loves them,' Tom said over her shoulder.

Surprised by his sudden appearance and the mention of his personal life, Perdy smiled warmly. 'The shows got great reviews, I'd like to see it sometime,' she remarked.

'We're in luck, Joe's got the drinks in,' Tom said, pointing to a table near the fireplace.

To Perdy's delight, a newspaper photo of Ryan and his spaniel had been placed next to her fruit juice. 'Family's stolen dog mysteriously reappears,' she read with a pang of guilt.

'Great piece, I thought you'd like to see it,' Joe said.

'Thanks. I didn't think it would be your sort of story.'

'Why? Because I'm a cynical hack incapable of being moved by a heartwarming feature.'

'That's not what I meant,' Perdy said in an unconvincing voice.

'How did you get on at the children's home?' Tom asked, changing the subject.

'A complex situation, the missing children weren't the only victims of grooming. The care worker was targeted online by a bloke trying to gain access to the boys. What's more, he used the same seduction technique to infiltrate Shotley Park children's home.'

'Sounds like organised crime,' Tom said, 'probably part of a County Lines gang. Did you inform the police?'

'Yes. They're really interested in pursuing the case.'

'A bloody miracle,' Joe retorted. 'When I was writing a feature about Somali boys groomed for drug trafficking, they turned a deaf ear.'

'Let's hope they find the missing teenagers before they become core gang members,' Tom said. 'One of the Somali lads was dealing heroin after a couple of weeks. When he tried to break away, he got stabbed in the stomach by another youth.'

'There's been a 50% increase in trafficked children being used to carry drugs,' Perdy stated.

'That doesn't surprise me. There are 27 County Lines operating from London to Norfolk alone,' Tom replied.

'Listen to us talking shop, that's what killed my marriage,' Joe moaned.

'That and a lot of other things,' Tom said affectionately. 'More comedy club tonight, is it?'

'Actually, it's performance poetry at Rich Mix.'

Perdy nearly laughed until she realised Joe was deadly serious. 'Now that's my kind of evening,' she said.

'Come with me, boost my morale for my hour upon the stage.'

'I'd like to,' she replied, 'but I'm visiting a friend who's just had a baby.'

'Pity, you'll miss my performance debut.'

'What's your poem about?' Perdy asked softly.

'It's in praise of my wife's divorce party. She did completely the right thing leaving me and I'm man enough to say it. What kind of plonker puts a job before his marriage?'

'And on that note, I'm going home,' Tom said. 'It's my turn to rustle up an evening meal.'

The men's candour amplified Perdy's feeling of shame, she'd told a white lie for no good reason to two trusted colleagues. 'I'll walk with you to the bus stop,' she said directly to Tom.

Joe had his head down, scrutinising his poem.

'You'll be great,' Perdy called out to attract his attention.

'That's the aim,' he quipped, with a twinkle in his sea-green eyes.

'Why am I trudging back to an empty flat when I could be having a blast listening to performance poetry?' Perdy asked Rocco.

'Only you can answer that. Do you remember the time we tried to smuggle Rita into the jazz club?'

'That was a long time ago. I'm incapable of having fun anymore.'

'Don't get lost behind the clouds, show your sunshine.'

'What if I'm so busy enjoying myself that I forget you?'

'That's impossible. I'm the smiling moon over a silvery lake.'

'Like the one we saw when we were skinny dipping?'

To Perdy's alarm, the loud screeching of car tyres drowned out Rocco's reply.

'Bloody idiot, watch where you're going,' an irate driver shouted from his vehicle.

'I'm sorry,' Perdy spluttered.

On the safety of the pavement, she looked around her with heightened awareness. Dick was walking up the road with the troubled girl she'd met outside the greengrocers. Knowing their circumstances, a surge of pity welled up in her heart for both of them.

It was a nice touch, Joe placing the photo by my drink, Perdy thought as she passed a bustling pub. She pictured him performing his poem with aplomb to a supportive audience. *Joe's a brave bloke stepping out of his comfort zone. Not many men could wear their heart on their sleeve in public.*

As she turned into her street, the chilling screams of a child in distress prompted Perdy to burst into a sprint.

'Oh my God, it's my brother,' she heard a girl call out despairingly.

By the time Perdy reached the scene, a boy was lying on the ground in a pool of cherry-red blood.

A hyped-up teenager bounced on the balls of his feet brandishing a knife. 'I had no choice,' he yelled to the sobbing girl.

'You fucking moron,' she screamed back, 'he's dying, Frank.'

'I'm sorry, sis,' the boy hollered before bolting down a passageway.

Perdy trembled at the sight of the girl bent over the injured youth.

'Keep the pressure on the wound,' Dick said calmly, 'the ambulance is on its way.'

'It's too late,' the girl cried in anguish. 'He's already dead and my brother's killed him.'

Chapter 16

An image of Rocco's blood-soaked bandana against his neck flashed into Perdy's mind.

'Take the poor child to the bus shelter until the police arrive,' Dick instructed.

Anxious to escape the tragic scene, Perdy placed her jacket around the girl's bare shoulders and led her away.

The faint smell of urine wafting around the shelter intensified Perdy's desire to vomit. She sat down beside the distraught girl on a thin plastic seat. 'What's your name?' she asked.

'Vicky,' the girl mumbled in a barely audible voice.

'Have you spoken to your brother since I last saw you?'

'No, I can't get anywhere near him thanks to Kevin.'

'Does he respond to your messages.'

'Not anymore. Frank's not the loving brother he used to be.'

'He's in the clutches of dangerous criminals.'

'I should have looked after him better. I'm a shit sister.'

'No, you're not. We can't control what happens to other people.'

'I've got to tell the police I saw Frank stab the boy.'

'Did you witness the incident?'

'Yes, but I was too far away to intervene.'

'The emergency services will be here soon,' Perdy said, looking over at the boy's dead body.

'Mam told me to look after Frank, I have to find him,' Vicky cried in a woeful voice.

'You've no idea where he's gone. He could be anywhere.'

Pumped with adrenaline, Vicky jumped up from her seat and darted towards the passageway used by Frank.

'Take care,' Perdy called out, fearing for the girl's safety in the vicious underworld.

A skateboarder oozing vitality weaved around the people surveying the crime scene. Not for the first time, Perdy contemplated the tragedy of young life being cut short. She was about to wave to Dick when a ghoulish onlooker stepped in front of him to take a photo of the dead body.

'Clear off,' Dick said assertively like a protective parent.

Seeing Perdy alone without the girl, he looked at her with a puzzled expression on his face.

'Vicky's gone to look for her brother,' Perdy explained when she reached him.

'I'll let the police know. Get yourself home, there are enough people helping here.'

'Only if you're sure,' Perdy said, feeling guilty about leaving Dick.

She had only taken a couple of steps when the sound of a siren rooted her to the spot. With a thumping heart, she recalled the air ambulance hovering over Rocco's dead body like a giant bird of prey. '*So much grief awaiting the boy's family,*' Perdy lamented as she trudged homewards.

The bushy-tailed foxes on the pram caught her attention before she realised Jeannie was pushing it. 'It's great to see you,' Perdy said warmly. 'I can't believe you've just given birth; you look amazing.'

'I don't feel it. I've been up through the night feeding this little guzzler.'

Jeannie pulled back the sky-blue blanket for Perdy to see her newborn son. Not the scrunched-up creature she was expecting, the baby was soft and plump with a mass of black hair. 'He's adorable,' Perdy said to her fatigued friend.

'I won't be having another one anytime soon. The birth was horrendous in more ways than one.'

'Oh, poor you.'

'Billy passed out in the delivery room when I was given an epidural. One minute he was holding my hand and the next he was on the floor.'

'Who says women are the weaker sex?'

'Dads collapsing during labour is more common than people think.'

At least you were both present at the birth, Perdy thought, recalling her own entry into the world. 'I've knitted Stanley a matinee jacket,' she said, 'I'll pop it round when you're ready for visitors.'

'My house has been like Clapham Junction. The firstborn grandchild gets a lot of adulation.'

Perdy smiled at the beauty of normality. 'It's cheered me up no end seeing both of you,' she said, giving Jeannie a tight hug.

'Let's meet up for coffee again soon. You can let me know how your job's going and I can bore you rigid with baby talk.'

'That's what good friends are for.'

'Take care,' Jeannie said as she set off down the road in the purple twinge of twilight.

'You too,' Perdy called out, aware of the growling pang of hunger in her stomach.

Walking back to her flat, she noted the plethora of fast food shops and was pleased she'd purchased fresh ingredients to cook at home. She envied Tom preparing a meal for his husband and wondered if one day she'd have someone special to dine with. *Maybe I'll invite Joe over for a tomatoey puttanesca packed anchovies and olives,* she thought as she neared the greengrocers.

A burly-looking man with a shaved head was carrying boxes of sweet potatoes into the shop. Something about his furtive look suggested he was delivering more than one kind of Jamaican produce.

Perdy took out her phone and looked at the street names to imply she was using Google Maps. When the man emerged hurriedly from the greengrocers, he barely noticed her standing in the shadows. Steadying himself with one hand, he jumped into the van and began collecting boxes from the rear of the vehicle.

Surreptitiously, Perdy slipped into the shop and hid under a grubby counter. A sizeable spider scuttling around her feet made her heart race. Afraid of squealing aloud, she squashed the fast-moving creature with the heel of her shoe.

The front door banged to a close, amplifying the terror she had inflicted on herself.

A man spoke with dickhead swagger: 'Bring the boxes over here. I want to count the packages before we take them down to the cellar.'

His mate made a kissing sound like an orangutan. 'Fucking sweet potatoes alright. 85 kilos of cocaine and cannabis all the way from Kingston Jamaica.'

'Mm, neat, sealed packages of money-making drugs.'

To Perdy's horror, she discerned a cat with big, intense eyes padding towards her.

'Thought I told you to get rid of that moggy before the old witch comes looking for her,' a voice snapped.

'You're right, I'll put her out. We don't want anyone seeing our secret hoard.'

'Not if they want to stay alive,' the boss man said demonically.

Bile from Perdy's stomach seeped into her mouth. 'Help me, Rocco, help me,' she pleaded over and over.

A hand descended towards the cat but the agile feline leapt artfully out of view.

'Stay perfectly still until those men go down to the cellar,' Rocco said, 'they're batshit crazy and so are you.'

Chapter 17

There was something deranged in the way the men began counting the packages. A levity in their voices showed total disregard for the severity of their crime. They could have been proclaiming the number of sweets they'd acquired on a profitable Halloween night.

'94 packages of cocaine and cannabis waiting to hit the streets,' one of them said, smugly. 'Help me take this lot down to the cellar. And put that bloody cat out.'

Perdy reflected on the number of lives that would be ruined by the sizeable haul: *Do any of the users stop to think about the people being killed to feed their habit?* she questioned.

A man stepped perilously close to the counter. 'Gotcha!' he called out in a cruel voice.

Nauseous with panic, Perdy curled up in a tight ball and closed her eyes. In the darkness, the long drawn-out meow of the cat in distress sounded louder and more disturbing. When the door creaked open, Perdy pictured the fearful tabby being tossed roughly out of the shop.

'Lock that now mate,' a man ordered. 'Frank's sister's hanging around and she's a pain in the arse. Thinks her brother's too good for the likes of us.'

'Not now he isn't. He's a murderer with blood on his hands.'

'Where is he by the way?'

'In Norwich, lying low until we need him again.'

Distraught, Perdy realised she was trapped in the greengrocers for the night with two depraved villains. 'What if they find me?' she asked Rocco.

'Keep your nerve, they won't even know you're here.'

'No one knows I'm here. I could be joining you in the afterlife, bloodied and battered by senseless thugs.'

'You're not helping yourself,' Rocco said. 'When they're down in the cellar, look for a better place to hide.'

The men started singing, 'Money, money, money' by Abba as if it was a well-rehearsed party piece.

Truly bonkers, Perdy thought. *Maybe they didn't have the presence of mind to remove the key from the door.*

Outside, the black night descended like a deathly coffin lid, intensifying her fear. Hunched in the tiny space, she dug her nails hard into the palm of her hand to focus her mind. *Why are the men taking such a long time to secrete their booty in the cellar?* she wondered. When their hideous singing ended, Perdy realised they were snorting cocaine in the back room. She wished she had a superpower and could confront the drug-addled scumbags but in reality, she was too afraid to move.

The squeaking of the cellar door alerted Perdy to the change in the men's whereabouts. With a burst of cocaine-fuelled energy, they began shifting the boxes of potatoes below ground. Perdy's head went into a spin as she sifted through pertinent questions: *Did the common vegetables still harbour 94 packages of drugs or had the crooks seized them for distribution? Were the men the puppet masters at the top of the supply chain who had orchestrated the boy's death?* Clearing her mind, she resolved to act immediately they took the last boxes to the cellar.

When all was quiet, Perdy surmised that the men were fully occupied stashing their cargo out of sight. Carefully, she shuffled backwards out of the cramped space and used the light from her mobile phone to locate the shop door. No magic key was dangling from the lock to herald her escape. *I desperately need somewhere to hide for the night before the wired-up men resurface.*

Aware that the floorboards were rattling, Perdy crept past the onions and garlic into the dingy back room. Adjusting her eyes, she searched quickly for a stock cupboard or a secluded recess she could slip into. The sight of a bunch of keys propped against the weighing scales triggered Perdy to change her mind. She grasped the bundle of metal in her hand and quickly selected a key to try in the door.

The heavy tread of the men walking up the stairs made her heart pound. Perdy had stepped within reaching distance of the shop entrance and realised it was too late to hide. With the skill of a medic racing against time, she inserted the mortice key into the lock. It turned easily so she reached up to the sturdy bolt keeping the door shut. Free moving at first, it jammed halfway across the plate causing Perdy's muscles to tremble. The sound of footsteps drawing closer escalated her panic but she resolutely prised the bolt through the metal box.

'Holly shit, it's the fucking journalist from across the road,' a man cried out as a light went on. He pounced forward to grab Perdy but she ran from his grimy hands into the street.

Late-night revellers, unsteady on their feet, were spilling out of the pub onto the pavement. Afraid for her safety, Perdy mingled with the men in their beer-stained shirts waiting for a taxi. She glanced back at the greengrocers and saw a hooded man emerge from the premises with long, menacing strides. *The mobster's out for my blood, if he catches me before I reach the police station I'm doomed.*

'Do you want to come home with me darling?' an obese bloke called out to her, in front of his girlfriend.

Ignoring his boorish comment, Perdy stepped behind a group of drunken people crossing the road. *I need to make a run for it before the drug-fuelled gangster stabs me in the back.* With adrenalized swiftness, she turned away from her flat and raced towards the park.

In the gloomy darkness, the trees lining the path looked spookily oppressive. *Is the malevolent gangster gaining pace behind me or have I thwarted his mission to kill?*

Caught up by nightmarish thoughts, she tripped over a fallen branch and tumbled to the ground. Prostrate on the path with gravel cutting into her hand, she heard someone running towards her.

Hopeful of rescue, Perdy looked up and discerned the fast-approaching figure of the hooded man. She realised the villain had outwitted her and accessed the park from the far end.

'Help, help!' she screamed as the cunning predator increased his speed.

Dick rose from a nearby bench. 'I'm coming,' he called out, gallantly.

'Thank the Lord!' Perdy exclaimed as she scrambled to her feet.

In a murderous mood, the psyched-up gangster whipped out a knife and pointed it viciously at Perdy. Dick stormed at the man like a raging bull and punched him hard in the face. The assailant dropped his weapon and staggered backwards into a thorny bush.

Perdy grabbed a strong twig from the grass and poked him in the eye.

The thug bellowed like an injured animal, 'I can't see. I can't see.'

Perdy flipped his palm up, then twisted his hand and forced it to the ground.

Dick kicked the villain in the groin before leaping on top of him to staple down his arm. The man pushed his head forward with great force but Dick grasped it tightly, impeding his movement.

'You've got him!' Perdy exclaimed with tears in her eyes.

'Call the police, tell them we've caught the scumbag.'

'It's their lucky day. He's a cut-throat gangster with a huge haul of drugs,' Perdy said, triumphantly.

'Watch out,' Dick called with heart-stopping terror in his voice.

Perdy turned to see the burly bloke from the greengrocers running hell-for-leather in her direction. 'Oh, My God,' she screamed, 'he'll crucify me.'

Spurred to action, she raced across the bowling green towards the dell with its cluster of thickset bushes. The marauding villain chased after her at ferocious speed.

He's gaining on me Rocco, if he catches me, I'm done for.

'Perdy power!' Rocco shouted encouragingly.

Buoyed on by his support, Perdy sharpened her focus to hurry down the mossy steps to the dell. At the bottom, her foot slipped into a deep hole in the ground, lurching her forward. She grabbed an overhanging branch and managed to steady herself before it snapped off the tree.

Vigilantly, she stepped towards the shrubbery concealing the vital park exit. An eerie snorting sound alerted her to the presence of an encroaching creature. *At least the gangster's too big to squeeze through the undergrowth*, Perdy assured herself as she prised through the bushes.

Scratched and stung, she pressed forward until the sudden yanking of her ponytail toppled her backwards. Unable to see her assailant, she felt for his hand and dug her nails in hard, like a seething animal. When the grip on her hair loosened, Perdy plunged into the shrubbery, away from the vicious thug.

Safely through the park exit, she visualised Dick sitting on top of the bloke's drug-addled mate. Aware that her friend was in immense danger, she quickly phoned the police.

'We're already on the case,' an officer said. 'Vicky called to let us know Dick had caught the gangster and a second was on the loose.'

Astounding, Perdy thought, *Vicky was probably in the park searching for her brother.*

'We've been after these men for a long time,' the officer said. 'They're part of a criminal gang which ensnares young people into selling drugs imported from Jamaica.'

'I'll make my way down to the station,' Perdy said, 'I'd like to make a statement.'

'Great,' the officer replied, 'you've been extremely brave.'

Perdy watched the star-studded outline of Rocco's face form in the inky black night. 'Phew, that was close!' he said, admiringly.

Chapter 18

'Tom's told me everything,' Joe said as he opened his lunch box. 'I can't believe you took such a risk.'

'Neither can I,' Perdy disclosed. 'There were times when I was scared for my life.'

'No story's worth getting killed for. These men are lethal criminals.'

'The drugs collectively weighed more than 85.5 kilos and would have been worth more than 35 million if sold on the streets.'

'And they were stashed away in boxes of sweet potatoes?'

'Yes, they were flown into Gatwick airport and collected from an industrial estate in Hayes.'

'Have all the drug dealers been caught?' Joe asked with an earnest expression on his face.

'They have. An analysis of the blokes' phones led the police to the smuggler who had links to Jamaica.'

'You need to take care; these gangsters still operate from prison.'

A feeling of dread assailed Perdy. 'Joe, you're frightening me,' she said.

'I'm telling it like it is, that's what journalists do. There's a spare bedroom at mine if ever you need to use it.'

'Hopefully, it won't come to that,' Perdy said, feigning a smile.

She watched Joe start to eat his man-sized sandwich with gusto. The lettuce and tomatoes on her plate reminded Perdy of the terrifying events in the greengrocers. She retched loudly, causing a lady to hurry past to a different part of the canteen. *Joe probably thinks I'm mad*, Perdy said to herself as she pushed away her food.

Lost in their own private thoughts, neither of them disrupted the ensuing silence. A big part of Perdy wanted to race back to the office to begin writing her feature but she lingered in Joe's company.

'How was your performance at the poetry club?' she asked, resuming the conversation.

'I was well out of my comfort zone but the audience seemed to enjoy it. It was one of the challenges I set myself during a coaching session.'

Perdy was taken aback by Joe's candour. 'Good for you, baring your soul,' she said.

'Everyone in the street went to Gemma's divorce party. The poem was a wry apology for ruining our marriage.'

'Are you still in touch with your ex-wife?'

'I am, Gemma's not the sort to bear grudges.'

'What made you start the coaching?'

'I had issues to confront. Next time I'm in a relationship, I don't want to be such a work-obsessed moron.'

'It's an easy trap to fall into,' Perdy said. 'I need more balance in my life.'

'Don't let the job rob you of the fun times. You should come to the comedy club on Saturday night.'

'I'm going back to Tyneside for the weekend, my parents are having a party.'

'I've never been to North East England, parts of it look amazing.'

'If you like beautiful architecture, canny people and unspoilt beaches, it's worth a visit,' Perdy said proudly.

'Why are you living in London? Get yourself back there.'

'Regional press has had its day, it's not the powerhouse it used to be.'

'You're right, it doesn't grapple with the big issues anymore.'

'The Newcastle Chronicle used to be a leading paper with real political clout.'

'It's the age-old dilemma,' Joe remarked. 'Do you live in a place you love or somewhere you can do important work?'

'Hope I've made the right choice,' Perdy said looking anxiously at the clock.

'You can't let your talent go to waste, just don't get killed chasing a story.'

Perdy laughed despite the gravity of Joe's warning. 'No more stoking a viper's nest,' she promised as she packed away her untouched salad.

On the train, Perdy sat in the quiet coach listening to Desert Island Discs on her earbuds. She recalled a feature in The Spectator that referred to Lauren Laverne as 'lightweight and uncerebral.' *It's probably because she's a modern Sunderland lass who speaks with a slight regional accent. Typical media prejudice against a bright and empathetic Northerner.*

Perdy admired the way Lauren gave the interviewee time to connect with her innermost thoughts. The war journalist spoke with deliberation about the fulfilment she got from her job: 'Seeing the brutality of war, I'm reminded of how lucky I am to have a family and a home to return to.'

Perdy was hit by the sunshiny essence of the woman pouring down the airwaves. She wanted to text Joe to tell him to listen to the programme but she realised that would be crossing a line.

Instead, Perdy turned to Rocco, 'I've been so wrapped up in my work, I've neglected my parents,' she said.

'They're adults, they don't need you checking on them every five minutes.'

'Things haven't been the same between us since I dropped out of medicine.'

'You've got a better relationship with your parents now than you've ever had.'

'I know I've been a disappointment to them.'

'Don't start catastrophizing. You simply changed direction and found your own way.'

'With a little help from my friend.'

'Reminds me of the Beatles song, a perfect disc to play on a desert island.'

'To stave off the loneliness, I would choose "I just called to say I love you" by Stevie Wonder,' Perdy said.

A couple of loud Glaswegians staggered into the quiet coach with bargain booze carrier bags. Perdy's heart sank when the drunken men spotted the vacant seats opposite her. With the histrionics of a comedy duo, they plonked their shopping on the table and peered at the reservation sign. They took so long staring at the electronic information that Perdy wondered if they could read. Eventually, after a garbled conversation filled with expletives, the men retrieved their booze and shuffled away.

To Perdy's relief, two laid-back students settled into the seats with youthful ease. She looked through the window at the expanse of shamrock green countryside and felt the thrill of escaping the urban sprawl.

'I like your blazer,' the blonde girl with a pixie haircut told her friend.

'It's from Oxfam. I haven't bought anything new in ages.'

'I still go shopping with my nan,' the girl said. 'We don't buy much but we love looking at the colour trends.'

Perdy recalled going to Tammy Girl with her grandma and buying a bright orange blouse with ruffles down the front. *Life's duller without her*, Perdy thought, *she had the knack of brightening every day. Even a cup of tea in Marks and Spencer was a special event when she was around.*

'It's a pity my mum won't get to be a grandma,' Perdy told Rocco. 'She might be like the husband hunting Mrs Bennet in Pride and Prejudice but no one can replace the man in my dreams.'

Chapter 19

Glad to be back in the sanctuary of her family home, Perdy patted the living room walls. *People will think I'm mad loving a house*, she told herself, *but Lyndhurst brought me such solace in difficult times, it holds a special place in my heart.*

Speculating where her father would be, Perdy strolled through the galley kitchen into the garden. She watched with filial affection as he tended the giant orange roses overlooking the sundial. For a fleeting moment, Perdy thought the cat sprawled out on the stone wall was Holly resurrected from her tiny grave. She remembered vividly how her independent pet became a lap-loving moggy in her old age. Through the veil of time, the sound of Holly's ecstatic purring as she sat on a velvet dressing gown, rang in her ears.

'Hi, Dad,' Perdy called out to attract the attention of her preoccupied father.

He perked up like a freshly watered plant. 'Hello, sweetheart,' he said, 'it's wonderful to see you.'

Perdy wrapped her arms around his frail body. 'You look well,' she told him kindly. 'I love the garden, such an array of colour.'

'I try my best. Unfortunately, the wind battered the yellow irises, they didn't last long.'

'Nothing you can do to control the North East weather, Dad. Where's Mum by the way?'

'She's just popped out to buy a few more things for the party. If you ask me, it's all a bit OTT. There aren't that many guests.'

'Who's coming beside the neighbours?' Perdy asked, fearful of the answer.

'A few people from the camera club and James Tyler, our new GP.'

'As in James Tyler who was in my sixth form?' Perdy said brusquely.

'Yes, I think so.'

Perdy saw the embarrassed look on his face. 'Oh, come on Dad, you know it's him,' she snapped. 'Mum's crossed a line this time, inviting a self-important nerd from my school days to her soirée.'

'She means well,' her father said, packing away his gardening tools.

'When will Mum get it into her head that I don't want a boyfriend and certainly not one chosen by her. So far, I've endured a dull accountant from Whitley Bay who wanted to know how much I was earning, a vet who didn't bother to change out of his work clothes and smelt of pig, and a lawyer who spent the evening cross-examining me like I was in the dock.'

'I think you'll find James good company,' her father said. 'He's a very popular GP.'

'He must have changed,' Perdy said in a scoffing voice. 'He bored everyone rigid at school. James Tyler once asked me how I'd done in a chemistry exam and when I said, "Surprisingly well", he looked disappointed.'

'I'll make sure he doesn't bother you too much,' her father said to Perdy's annoyance.

'I don't need you to protect me from a fixated jobsworth with zilch personality,' she replied.

'I've made a playlist for the party with some of your favourite tracks on,' her father said, diverting the conversation.

'I'm not sure what the neighbours will make of Billie Eilish but they'll love Beyoncé and Sam Fender,' Perdy said with a smile.

'Your mum shouldn't be too long now hinny. In fact, I think that's her pulling onto the drive.'

Perdy seized the opportunity to talk candidly to her father. 'Thanks for your helpful letter,' she said.

'I'm no good on the telephone and I wanted you to know how proud I am that you found your own way. I felt all along that medicine wasn't right for you but your mum thought otherwise. You were so precious to us after all the mishaps, I'm afraid we became helicopter parents.'

'It didn't help that my school marginalized the Arts and pushed the brightest students into the STEM subjects.'

'Or that it was a competitive, exam-driven academy. We should have ignored their brainwashing tosh and helped you discover your own talents.'

'I wish I'd had the guts to speak out.'

'We're all capable of letting our silences brew into a storm,' her father remarked. 'We did you wrong, not telling you about your birth.'

Perdy resisted the temptation to open an old wound.

'We all have to learn to dance in the rain, not hide indoors,' she said.

With perfect timing, her mother's lively voice called out from the bottom of the garden: 'Hi, darling, I hope you're looking forward to the party. My poor head's so overloaded, I've scraped the car on the wall.'

'Again!' Perdy and her father exclaimed in perfect unison.

'Sorry, Mike,' her mother said, prolonging her vowels in a childlike way.

'Why is it that every time I buy a new car, you christen it with a scratch?' he asked jokingly. 'I'll go and inspect the damage.'

Poor Mum, she's not the best driver, Perdy thought as she gave her a tight hug.

'I've bought you a present,' her mother said, producing a canary-yellow maxi dress from a Fenwick's bag.

Perdy was about to revert to the teenager who'd sneered at her birthday gift of a fuchsia pink raincoat. Instead, liking the feel of the viscose material, she held the garment against her. 'It's lovely, Mum, thank you,' she said. 'I think Africa's given me a taste for bold colours, the clothes are so joyful over there.'

'It's wonderful to see how much you've grown in confidence since you became a journalist.'

'Rocco and Fayola inspired me to find my calling,' Perdy said. 'It's strange how they came into my life.'

'So many things are beyond our comprehension,' her mother replied. 'After the muddle of your birth, I learned to override the questions and appreciate my blessings.'

'I've definitely got the right name; I have a habit of getting lost.'

'But what a joy when you were found and placed in my arms. Why don't you wear that beautiful dress tonight angel? You'll shine like the sun.'

At that exact moment, Rocco's smiling face appeared in a cloud that had detached itself from the sky and was perched on the rooftops.

'With any luck, the bright, gaudy dress will make James Tyler run a mile,' Perdy told him. 'Make sure you stay around for the party; I'll be needing you.'

Trailing behind her mother on the garden path, she blew Rocco a stealthy kiss. A jet-black crow swooped down from the apple tree to the half-eaten cherries on the ground, making her jump. Determined to be calm for evening shenanigans, Perdy took a long deep breath before going indoors.

Chapter 20

'Is there anything I can help you with before I take a stroll down to the Willows?' Perdy asked her mother.

'No, everything's under control, sweetheart. You go and make the most of your free time. I know how precious it is.'

'I certainly haven't inherited your baking skills,' Perdy said, eyeing the mouth-watering quiche on top of the stove.

'No one's good at everything, we all have our talents,' her mother replied.

'I'll second that,' her father said as he entered the room. 'The car's not too bad by the way, just a light scratch this time.'

Perdy decided to make a quick exit before her father reiterated instructions on how to turn into a driveway.

'I'll take the shortcut through the graveyard down to the river. I won't be long,' she said.

Striding down to the Willows, Perdy noticed a spring in her step that eluded her when she walked in London. A mother stroking her baby's head under the oak tree made her think of Jeannie and her infant cooped up in the city. *'I want my children to grow up where they can run through fields in crisp, fresh air,'* Perdy told herself.

Glad to be on home turf, she hurried past the village green to the cobbled path leading to the church. Since childhood, the Gothic building with its octagonal tower spiralling up to the sky had seemed magical to her. Perdy wanted to sit on a bench and savour the atmosphere of the place, not rush away to a tiresome party.

Despite being on a tight schedule, she trod slowly over the stony track which sloped down to the river. Awed by the mass of dark green trees surrounding her, she recalled Wordsworth's fitting line, *"The loveliest spot that man hath ever found"*.

Much to her delight, a fragile deer stepped briefly into view before bounding away into dense woodland. Struck by the beauty of the scene, Perdy lamented that she'd chosen a life disconnected from nature.

Behind the ferry house, the brownness of the River Tyne made it look like it was brim-full of pale ale. Perdy stayed clear of the level crossing whilst a long, noisy freight train rattled by. When the luminous green light appeared, she raced expectantly down to the waterfront.

The mighty Tyne stretched in front of her, peacefully uniting Newcastle and Gateshead without a trace of its industrial past. Perdy felt a stab of pride that her ancestors were keelmen who worked strenuously on the river in busier times. She pictured them in their stylish blue jackets and bell-bottom trousers, steering large coal-laden boats to waiting ships.

Eschewing the temptation to dally on the riverbank, Perdy took the sandy path up to the Willows. Apart from a dog walker heading towards Peth Lane, she had the undulating grassland to herself. A bright copper-coloured butterfly flitted erratically in front of her before alighting on a tall, pink weed. Sensing a change in the weather, she looked up at the wave-like clouds rippling in the sky.

'Mackerel sky, mackerel sky – never long wet, never long dry,' Perdy recited as she quickened her pace. To her amusement, the bulrushes standing rigid around the pond reminded her of sentinel guards in busby hats.

'Come and see the dragonflies,' a familiar voice called out from the water's edge.

Perdy stopped in her tracks. James Tyler was talking to a young girl crouched on the ground with a fishing net. She watched him lift the child high into the air so she had a better view of the radiant insects.

'They've come out of their homes under the water,' James said. 'We're lucky to see them.'

'They're moving so quickly all I can see is flashes of blue and green,' the girl told him.

Their warm intimacy piqued Perdy's curiosity. *Who is this child lovingly attached to James?* she wondered. Keen to find out, she stepped down the embankment to join them.

Iridescent dragonflies glided over the pond. 'Aren't they glorious,' Perdy said, softly.

James's beaming smile put paid to her notion that he was emotionally stunted.

'It's great to see you,' he said, 'your mum told me you were coming home for the party.'

'I'm looking forward to it,' Perdy replied, falsely.

'This is Bella,' James said, as he released the girl from his protective grasp. Her eyes still held the wonder of a spellbound child as her feet touched the ground. James watched her retrieve her fishing net before continuing to

106

speak. 'She's my sister's daughter,' he said. 'When her daddy died, it made sense for me to move back home.'

'Oh, poor Lucy. How's she coping?' Perdy asked.

'Not well, that's why I help out.'

The girl's gleeful giggles from the edge of the pond caught his attention. 'Bella's remarkable,' James said, 'she's a real blessing.'

'Mum tells me you're the local GP, good for you. I'm afraid I abandoned my plans to become a doctor.'

'You did the right thing. I've read your features, you're a born journalist.'

Perdy was startled that the saturnine sixth former of old took an interest in her work. Outgoing and complimentary, it was as if James had become a totally different person. 'We've both changed a lot since the sixth form,' she said with a laugh.

'I hope so, we were pretty awkward teenagers.'

In the ensuing silence, Perdy contemplated the rockiness of their shared youth when they'd struggled to be themselves. She marvelled that the tanned and athletic-looking GP standing by her side was her rival from school.

Aware that time was passing, 'I'd better go and help Mum get ready for the party,' she announced.

'I've been taking dancing lessons, I'll show you some moves later,' James said.

Perdy remembered them both at the sixth-form ball, gawkily watching others boogie the night away.

'A man of real surprises,' she said with a note of incredulity in her voice. 'I'll hunt out my dancing shoes, I haven't worn them in ages.'

Bella slung the fishing net over her shoulder and wiggled her tiny fingers to wave goodbye.

Perdy reciprocated the heartwarming gesture. 'Have fun,' she called out before turning homewards.

Chapter 21

After the conviviality of the weekend, Perdy felt unsettled in her spartan flat. Thwarted by a pang of loneliness, she stopped slicing the courgettes and reached for her phone. 'Hi, Mum, thanks for a brilliant weekend,' she said, surprised by the verity of her words.

'Did you enjoy the party?' her mother asked. 'You and James seemed to be having a great time together.'

Perdy disliked talking to her mother about personal matters but she answered candidly. 'I haven't enjoyed myself so much in ages, James was a hoot. He told me he went to his friend's wedding twice. Apparently, he was all spruced up in the church when an unexpected bride walked down the aisle. Mr "Not-Always-Perfect" had got the wrong date.'

'James needs a woman to take care of him,' her mother remarked, totally oblivious to the ridiculousness of her comment.

'He isn't a man-child, James is a competent GP,' Perdy heard herself saying.

'Do you think you'll stay in touch with him?'

'Yes, he was surprisingly easy to talk to,' Perdy said, without going into detail.

The depth of their conversation had taken her by surprise and was etched in her memory. She heard his words ringing in her ears: '*Dealing with sudden death catapults you into alien territory. You wake in a new land and scramble around trying to survive.*'

It was as if James had held up a mirror to my life and was echoing my sentiments, Perdy thought.

'Hi, sweetheart, are you still there?' her mother asked, in a loud voice.

'Yes,' Perdy answered.

'As I was saying, you looked beautiful in that bright yellow dress.'

Perdy recalled James giving her a similar compliment when they were strolling in the moonlit garden. 'The party really lifted my spirits,' she told her mother.

'That's wonderful, sweetheart, I'm so pleased.'

'Tell Dad I loved his playlist,' Perdy said as she looked through her window at the greengrocers. To her surprise, Vicky was outside the shop, pacing up and down like a lost soul. 'Sorry, Mum, I need to go now. Something's come up.'

'Take care,' her mother called out in a worried voice.

Perdy grabbed her cardigan and raced down the communal stairs to speak to Vicky.

'Hi,' she said gently to the troubled girl, 'any news about your brother?'

'None whatsoever, that's why I'm here.'

'Thanks for ringing the police, they've got the drug dealers in custody.'

'Did you tell them Frank stabbed that poor boy?'

'I answered all their questions. Your brother needs to turn himself in so he can get help.'

'And you think that's what he'd get? He's killed a boy.'

'We've got the evidence that Frank was groomed,' Perdy stated. 'He's a victim himself.'

'If I'd told the police earlier, Frank could have been protected. Now he's a murderer.'

'None of this is your fault, these gangs are clever at manipulating people. If Frank turns himself in, mitigating circumstances will be taken into account. Has he got any previous convictions?'

'No, Mum kept him on the straight and narrow. All she ever wanted was us to do well at school and make something of our lives.'

'I'm pleased you're still studying; it takes real strength to focus when your life gets torn apart.'

'I have to find Frank before he ends up dead,' Vicky declared.

Or kills again, Perdy said to herself.

'What happened to the other boys who were living in the greengrocers?' Vicky asked.

'Fortunately for them, they've been safeguarded by the police.'

'I thought they wouldn't see Frank as a victim, that's why I didn't go to them.'

'Is that the only reason?' Perdy enquired.

'No, the men said they'd kill me and Frank if I went to the police.'

Out of the corner of her eye, Perdy saw a white van driving towards them on the wrong side of the road. At the exact moment it swerved dangerously onto the pavement, she realised the driver's intention. 'Watch out,' Perdy screamed at the top of her voice as she pushed Vicky hard into a doorway.

The frenzied driver accelerated quickly towards Perdy but within an inch of her life, she leapt to safety.

'Bloody hell, that was close,' Vicky shrieked. 'Are you alright?'

'Just about,' Perdy said, her body shaking.

'Why was he trying to crash into us?' Vicky asked in a quavering voice.

'Revenge,' Perdy replied. 'I helped catch the drug dealers and now they're out for my blood.'

Shaken by the incident, they sat in silence for a while before Vicky resumed their conversation.

'I recognised the van; it belongs to the guitar teacher who gave Frank his lessons.'

'I'm surprised he isn't in police custody. He played a pivotal role in grooming young boys for drug dealing.'

'He's got a young daughter with beautiful red hair. She came with him once to the children's home.'

Perdy recalled the girl selling drugs in broad daylight to people impervious of her plight. 'I think I'll be paying the police another visit. The musician's clearly a key member of the drugs network,' she said.

'Aren't you frightened?' Vicky asked with concern in her eyes.

'Not when there's a job to be done, like finding your brother.'

'I don't know where to start and I've got an exam tomorrow.'

'What is it?' Perdy asked.

'Maths, it's one of my strongest subjects.'

'It used to be one of mine, there's something gratifying about problem-solving. I suggest you concentrate on your schoolwork and leave the sleuthing to me.'

'Thanks,' Vicky said, stifling a sob.

'Frank's lucky to have a sister like you,' Perdy told the gutsy teenager. 'Make sure you smash that exam tomorrow.'

Chapter 22

'That driver was out to get you,' Rocco said frankly. 'You can't stay in your flat tonight.'

'What do you suggest I do, go back to Tyneside and run away from it all?' Perdy said.

'Go to Joe's, he's offered you use of his spare room.'

'He's a work colleague, it could get awkward.'

'In what way? Am I missing something?'

Perdy relived the horror of the van mounting the pavement and driving straight towards her. *Joe was right,* she reflected, *the drug dealers are still orchestrating violence from behind bars.*

'Is there anywhere else you can stay other than Joe's?' Rocco asked.

'No,' Perdy said swiftly. 'Dick's got enough on his plate and I'm not exposing Jeannie to danger.'

She looked across at her flat. The cheese plant pressed against the window seemed to be warning her to keep away. *It's the obvious place to stage an attack on a solo woman, I can't go back there.*

'Ring Joe,' Rocco coaxed.

With a sense of urgency, Perdy dialled Joe's personal phone number for the very first time. When he didn't pick up, her surroundings appeared to become eerily strange and unfamiliar. She leant against the shopfront and forced herself to ring again.

'Hi, Perdy, is everything alright?' Joe asked immediately he answered his phone.

'I was wondering if I could stay at yours for the night,' she said.

'The offer of the spare room still stands but I'm on a date at the moment,' Joe replied. 'The evening's been a drag, I'll make my escape as soon as I can.'

'Thanks, Joe, you're a lifesaver.'

'I'll text you the address and directions from Finsbury Park tube station. I hope you haven't been stoking a viper's nest.'

'Believe you me, I've been keeping my head down but there was an incident with a van. I'll tell you about it when I see you.'

'I look forward to some intelligent conversation,' Joe said with a sigh. 'Bye, Perdy.'

Immensely relieved, she watched a girl with beautiful red hair run down the road towards a man. He placed his arm firmly around her shoulder like a protective father. *It's the bastard who tried to run me over*, Perdy realised with a feeling of dread. *Why is he lingering in the vicinity with the child?*

Anxious to get away, she raced upstairs to her flat to grab the packed case she'd used at the weekend. *Calm down*, Perdy told herself. *The man's not going to do anything with his daughter around.* Not sure how long she would be at Joe's, she seized a fistful of underwear from a drawer and dropped it in her tote bag. As she turned out the lights, a stab of sadness about leaving her home took Perdy by surprise.

In the street, the van which had careered towards her was brazenly visible. With the sweet red-headed girl by his side, the man was coercing women out of the barbershop into the vehicle. Perdy looked on in disbelief. *It can't be more trafficking; this isn't a district in southern Mexico.*

Before she could dart out of view, the man noticed her taking an interest in the disquieting scene. He looked her straight in the eye and made a throat-slitting gesture with his tattooed hand.

As he drove manically away, Perdy confronted the grim reality of the situation. *That thug's a nasty piece of work, the women were clearly terrified of him.* Unable to shake off her concern for their welfare, she crossed the road to check out the barbershop.

Through the window, Perdy viewed an unremarkable room furnished with two rows of chairs and uniform mirrors. The property was clean and tidy, except for a crumpled-up coat on the wooden floor. Perdy was on the verge of turning away when a ripple of movement caught her attention. A dog stirring, was her initial thought until big human eyes peered out from beneath the coat. Dumbfounded, she watched a petite Filipino woman emerge from the covering like a cautious animal.

Not wanting to startle her, Perdy knocked gently on the window to attract her attention.

The woman jerked her head upwards and smiled as if sighting a precious friend. Although her face was etched with sorrow, there was a child-like joy in her expression. Without any possessions and slipper-like shoes on her feet, she ran to the door.

'Please God, let it open,' Perdy said, recalling her own hair-raising exit from the greengrocers.

In no time at all, the woman stepped emotionally from the barbershop onto the pavement. 'Thank you for coming,' she said with a rush of happiness.

'Those women getting into the van looked so wretched, I wanted to check the place out,' Perdy told her.

'I thought you'd come to help me escape,' the woman said in a panicky voice.

Perdy looked steadfastly into her dark brown eyes. 'Escape from what?' she asked.

'Being forced to clean and wash dishes from 5 in the morning to midnight, 7 days a week.'

'Domestic servitude.'

'When my husband was sick and couldn't work, I used an agency to get a job in London.'

'But things didn't work out as you expected.'

'No, evil men took my passport and forced me to work long hours for little money.'

'And what about the other women, the ones I saw getting into the van?'

'We all came to England to help our families in the Philippines. Now we're trapped here like animals.'

'Where do you sleep?' Perdy asked, trying to unearth the facts.

'It used to be in the cellar but the women have been moved because the "pigs are poking around".'

'We need to act fast. When the driver realises you're missing, he'll be back to get you.'

The sound of a car door slamming made the women cling to each other in fright. With trepidation, they turned in unison to look at the vehicle.

'It's my friends from the Workers Association,' the woman cried out, 'they've come to rescue me!'

Chapter 23

'I've had enough of the dating scene,' Joe told Perdy as he cleared her plate away.

'Thanks, that curry was delicious,' she said, 'you're a talented cook.'

'I made it last night for my lonesome self, nothing like a decent meal to lift the spirits.'

'Well, that's lifted mine after such a fraught day.'

'I remember what it's like being a young reporter chasing every lead. Just don't fall into the trap of letting a job define who you are.'

'It's a big part of my life,' Perdy said. 'I want to be a good reporter.'

'What makes you so driven?' Joe asked, in a caring way.

Perdy was ready to open up about her past. It wasn't just Joe's sea-green eyes hooking her in, his kindness made her feel safe. 'A dear friend fuelled my passion for journalism when I was floundering in the dark,' she said.

'The man in the photograph on your desk?'

'What makes you ask that?'

'He's clearly someone very special to you and yet you never mention him.'

'His name's Rocco and he died in a tragic accident.'

'That puts the breakdown of my marriage into perspective, it must be hard losing someone you love.'

'Rocco intended to be a journalist. He lives on in my heart.'

'An inspirational soulmate.'

Perdy and Joe smiled at each other in a moment of hushed silence.

'How many dates have you been on since your divorce?' Perdy asked warmly.

'One and that was one too many,' Joe said in a solemn voice.

'It can't have been that bad.'

'It was like being on a date with a teenager; she photographed the meal, her drink and me looking pissed off.'

'Doesn't sound like your sort of lady, what made you go on the date in the first place?'

'I met her at the bar of the comedy club, I'd had that much to drink, she seemed like good company.'

'Being with someone you've got nothing in common with makes you feel more lonely,' Perdy said.

'Are you speaking from experience?'

'Not in the same way but when I was studying medicine, I felt alienated from the other students.'

'Good call making your way into journalism, you're one of the gang now.'

'Thanks for letting me stay, I didn't want to be alone in my flat tonight.'

'The sooner that van driver's behind bars, the better. Were the police responsive when you called at the station?'

'Yes, they're keen to interview the man on several accounts. It seems he's escalating up the criminal ladder.'

'It happens. People start off doing small jobs and reposition themselves with different gangs in bigger roles. Stay at mine until they've got the bastard.'

'I might take you up on that,' Perdy said gratefully.

'How did the police treat the Filipino woman?'

'She was backed by the Workers Association so they listened carefully to her story.'

'Domestic servitude is a rife form of modern slavery but it's difficult to detect. The police will be pleased to get a lead.'

'If the proposed bill becomes law, it will empower the traffickers and drive the victims underground,' Perdy said.

'It's shocking that the women paid an agency to get work in the UK.'

'They thought they were being recruited for the care sector, now they're strangled by debt and trapped in slave labour jobs.'

'It's your sort of story, I'm sure you'll do it justice. The spare room's ready if you want to hit the sack. Just to warn you, it's got vintage teddy bear wallpaper.'

'I didn't know you had a child.'

'I don't. It was up when we bought the house and because we were trying for a family, we didn't redecorate. Sadly, Gemma didn't get pregnant.'

Sensing that Joe was about to say more, Perdy stayed silent.

'It put a strain on our marriage and I handled the situation badly.'

'I'm sure you did your best.'

'Men have a lot to learn about being a supportive partner. I messed up big time.'

'Credit to both of you that you've managed to stay friends.'

'I won't be so selfish in my next relationship.'

'Do you fancy a supper drink?' Perdy said. 'You can tell me a few jokes before we go to bed.'

'Come with me to the comedy club, you'll love it.'

'It's a long time since I had a fun night out.'

'How about this for a joke? I hate it when someone spends four minutes telling you they don't have five minutes to speak to you.'

'Not bad,' Perdy said with a laugh.

The glow of sunrise streaked over the teddy bear wallpaper in Joe's spare room. Perdy wished a child was around to enjoy the sweetness of the vintage print. Thinking about her candid conversation with Joe, she realised he'd become more than just a work colleague. *He's a trusted friend,* she thought, *someone who's got my back in this shady city.*

Perdy didn't want to swan around Joe's house in her velvet dressing gown. To strike the right smart/casual balance for work, she put on high-waisted trousers and a burgundy blouse. When she looked in the free-standing mirror, Dolly Parton's song, '9-5' sprang into her mind. Unable to shake off the catchy tune, Perdy started singing it as she entered the kitchen.

'You worked a lot longer than that yesterday,' Joe said brightly.

'Don't remind me, I hope today's more straightforward.'

'I've put you a coffee and a croissant on the table. I'm just jumping in the shower.'

'A real treat, thanks.'

Perdy picked up the newspaper Joe had placed thoughtfully by her breakfast. On the front page, there was a photograph of a mother weeping for her dead son. Perdy began to read the news article: '*A 15-year-old was stabbed to death in Hackney on Thursday night. "Ezra was the sweetest boy, always positive, always smiling", his mother said.*'

Perdy realised Ezra was the boy Frank had stabbed to death in the street. *If Vicky sees this harrowing photograph of the victim's mother, it will tear her apart. I need* to *help her find Frank before he moves further up the criminal ladder.*

Perdy was diverted by Joe singing in the shower. *What's making him so happy?* she wondered. *He's belting out that love song.*

Chapter 24

Tom looked penetratively at Joe and Perdy when they entered the newsroom together. 'Everything alright?' he asked, with the instinct of a good journalist.

As if in a news briefing, Percy outlined the shocking events of the previous day.

'Just remember, your safety always comes first,' Tom said. 'I'm pleased you're staying at Joe's.'

'So am I,' Joe said in a manner that elicited a smile from Perdy.

Tom tilted his head as he spoke: 'How did your date go last night?' he asked.

'It was memorable for all the wrong reasons. She thought Angela Rayner was the leader of the Labour Party,' Joe replied.

'Maybe it was wishful thinking on her part,' Tom said.

Perdy was admiring the men's heartfelt camaraderie when her telephone rang. 'Hi, Jeannie, how's it going?' Perdy asked, disconcerted by the surprise call.

'Apart from the fact that I've become a milk machine, fine thanks.'

'Wonderful, I'll bring Stanley's present around soon.'

'I'm sorry to bother you at work but I promised Vicky I'd pass on a message. She was outside your flat last night, desperate to see you.'

'I'm staying with a friend at the moment,' Perdy said, without imparting any details.

'Vicky wants you to know that she sent Frank a link to the news article about the stabbing. He's going to meet her at Astwood Road Cemetery at 11 o'clock today. She wondered if you could be there.'

'I really appreciate you getting in touch Jeannie, you're a star.'

'Even in my sleep-deprived state, I sensed it was urgent.'

'If I leave now, I'll get there on time.'

'Take care,' Jeannie said, supportively.

In the colourful cemetery, awash with flowers, Perdy recalled placing white lilies on Rocco's grave. The words she had spoken in the midst of mourners rang in her ears: '*Good night, sweet prince, and flights of angels sing thee to thy rest.*'

Stepping past a boy and his grandad, Perdy overheard a snippet of their conversation: 'Are we in heaven?' the child asked.

'Not quite there yet,' the old man replied with a chuckle.

The sweetness of the exchange made Perdy smile even though her stomach was churning.

Aware of passing time, she surveyed the rambling maze of graves with a sinking heart. *I'll never find Vicky before 11 o'clock*, Perdy despaired as a lone figure stepped into view.

Recognising Frank with his distinctive blonde hair, Perdy knelt down beside a grave like a grieving widow. She watched him stride towards the freshly dug soil at the far end of the cemetery. With his scrawny, slumped shoulders and drooped head, he looked desperately forlorn. *It's a miracle the newspaper article galvanised him into action*, Perdy thought, *Vicky's prayers have been answered.*

Perdy followed Frank surreptitiously along the pathway to the newer graves. On high alert, she glanced around to check that evil thugs weren't hot on his tail. For a brief moment, the beautiful cemetery with its timeless grace quelled her anxiety.

Then suddenly, Frank broke into a sprint, jolting her back to reality. *Those villainous drug dealers won't let him get far*, she told herself.

A few steps further on, Perdy caught sight of Vicky waiting with open arms for her errant brother. She witnessed the siblings clasp each other tightly at the foot of a grave. After the embrace, Frank tousled Vicky's hair in an open display of affection.

Reluctant to intrude on their privacy, Perdy stayed in the background whilst they placed roses in a memorial vase. *Why are they taking such a long time?* she wondered. *Lethal predators could pounce on Frank at any moment.* When the siblings bowed their heads to pray over the grave, Perdy found herself petitioning God on their behalf.

To her alarm, she saw Frank step from his sister's side as if preparing to run away. Noticing the look of utter despair on Vicky's face, Perdy rushed forward to intercede. By the time she was on the scene, the conversation between the siblings was on a knife-edge.

'They've made it clear,' Frank said, 'if I go to the police, they'll kill you.'

'If you leave now, you'll kill me anyhow. I'm begging you, turn yourself in.'

'You've come this far, keep your courage,' Perdy said calmly to Frank.

'Mum's watching over you, draw strength from her love,' Vicky pleaded.

Frank continued to back away from her like an animal fearing captivity.

Perdy checked again for the presence of lurking hitmen but only a magpie was eyeing the scene.

Vicky ran towards Frank but before she could reach him, he dropped to his knees. 'Mum, please help me,' he cried out in anguish, 'I've killed a boy.'

Vicky wrapped her arms around her pitiful brother. 'Mum would want you to go to the police,' she coaxed. 'Do you want me to give them a ring?'

Frank lifted his tear-stained face. 'Yes, before those bastards find out where I am.'

'That's very brave,' Vicky said, placing her head tenderly next to his.

Afraid that Frank would change his mind, Perdy gestured to Vicky that she would make the vital call. In the background, she saw a second resplendent magpie fly past the siblings and land on their mother's grave. *Those we love never truly leave us,* Perdy assured herself as she grabbed her phone.

Chapter 25

'I'm pleased Frank went to the police,' Joe said in a sincere voice. 'If he tells them everything, somewhere down the line he'll be able to make a fresh start.'

'I hope so,' Perdy said. 'It must be hard to live with yourself when you've killed a man.'

'At least he broke away from those evil thugs, that's a miracle in itself.'

'The police rescued the Filipino women from a house in Camden. They've got the van driver in custody; I can go home now.'

Joe looked like a crestfallen child about to lose a playmate. 'Stay at mine for the night,' he suggested, 'I'll cook a meal and we can watch a film together.'

Perdy baulked at the idea of extending her stay in someone else's home. 'I need to make a start on my feature and I have some washing to do,' she said.

They both laughed at the lameness of her excuse.

'You can do some work whilst I beaver away in the kitchen,' Joe said teasingly. 'And I guess the washing can wait until another day.'

'We don't want to trigger office gossip,' Perdy remarked, 'Tom's antennae will detect a change in our relationship.'

'And what change might that be?' Joe asked. 'We're only friends hanging out together.'

Perdy smiled at the truth of his words. 'Put like that, it's an offer I can't refuse,' she said.

'Great, feel free to choose the film. I'm getting myself a beer, can I get you anything to drink?'

'A beer sounds tempting but I'll leave it for now,' Perdy said.

'What makes you so fearful of alcohol?' Joe asked gently.

'After Rocco's death, I guzzled vodka to anaesthetise the pain of losing him. It led me to a dark place.'

'Good for you turning things around, I wish I had your discipline and fortitude.'

'I hope Frank finds the strength to thrive again.'

'It sickens me that he was groomed in a children's home by someone he trusted.'

'Just like the Filipino women who put their faith in a bogus agency.'

'Listen to us talking shop, it's the road to ruin,' Joe said.

'We're discussing things that matter to us, it's the sort of conversation I enjoy,' Perdy told him.

'We could go the whole hog and choose a film set in a newsroom,' Joe said with a grin.

'How about "The Post" with Meryl Streep and Tom Hanks? It's definitely one of my favourites.'

'Mine too, I love it when journalists expose government deception.'

'A distant relative of mine was a GI bride; she lost her son in the Vietnam War.'

'What was her name?' Joe asked as if the story mattered to him.

'Frieda, she was my great grandma's sister,' Perdy said.

'Poor Frieda, her American dream turned into a nightmare.'

'She arrived in the country with such optimism and her son, like thousands of other men, was sacrificed in a futile war.' Remembering the harrowing words in Frieda's diary, tears welled up in Perdy's eyes.

Eager to soothe her distress, Joe reached out and touched her hand.

'Do you need any help in the kitchen?' Perdy asked to reciprocate his kindness.

'No, I'll be listening to the football on my radio – you can make a start on your work.'

Before knuckling down to her feature, Perdy read a message from James on her phone: 'The brilliant white Hawthorn blossom is out in the Willows, I wish you were here.'

A desperate yearning to be back in nature tugged at Perdy's heartstrings. She closed her eyes and pictured herself standing next to James under the lustrous blooms.

In her daydream, a boy picked up a sprig of blossom from the ground and gave it to her. '*Thanks, sweetheart,*' she said, as she took the delicate love token from his hand.

James placed his arm around her waist and together they watched the boy race full pelt to the pond. Beaming with delight, the child called out from the water's edge, '*Mum, Dad, come and see the dragonflies, they're beautiful.*'

Wanting to remain in her sweet dream, Perdy blocked out the words ringing in her ears. Eventually, Joe's cheery voice brought her back to the real world. 'How's the work going?' she heard him say.

'Not very well as you can see,' Perdy replied. She said nothing about her dream because it was intensely personal and precious to her.

'If I knock out the first draft of my feature, will you cast your expert eyes over it?' Perdy asked Joe.

'I'd love to but the meal's nearly ready. Leave your work until tomorrow, you've done enough for today.'

Perdy nodded in agreement. 'I'll find the film, I think it's on Netflix.'

'The house feels like a home again with you around,' Joe said as he handed her the remote.

His endearing words added to Perdy's gamut of conflicting emotions. 'What was that dream all about?' she asked Rocco when Joe returned to the kitchen.

'You're at a crossroads in life,' he said. 'Do you follow your heart or your head?'

The pull of home and an immense wave of love for James made Perdy gasp for breath. After an agonizing pause, she spoke from the core of her being: 'I've worked so hard to become a journalist, I can't abandon my dream job and return to Newcastle.'

'Wherever you go and whatever you do, I will always be watching over you.'

Perdy looked at the smiling moon illuminating the sky. 'I know dearest Rocco,' she said, 'in every season of my life you will be part of me.'

END